GOOD AT DRUGS

KKUURRTT

GOOD AT DRUGS

a novel

FESTIVALIA SCHEDULE

FRIDAY
12PM - They Have Come for
Our Minds
2PM - Brothersport
4PM - 111111115111
6PM - Dance Illusion ☾
8PM - Mistress Synth
10PM - Tripp Danielson
12AM - Nys Funk
2AM - AMAAAZING
4AM – Whizzard

SATURDAY
6AM - Control Logic ☼
8AM - Imaginary Animal
10AM - Lyle & Kyle
12PM - Cactus Snake
2PM - Jason J. Jackson Jr.
4PM - Bass Dimension
6PM - RBCCA ☾
8PM - T.U.R.B.o.
10PM - Paul McCartney II
12AM - The Beatles II
2AM - ??/Perhaps\??
4AM - Brunch (Lunch b2b
Mary Bloody)

SUNDAY
6AM - C'est Magnifique ☼
8AM - Pleasuredome
10AM - Nathaniel Chase
12PM - Bird Song
2PM - Copy Copy
4PM - The Kids
6PM - TST ☾
8PM - Derrick Carter B2B
Mark Farina
12AM - Love Language
2AM - TimeCop Presents:
Witching Hours
4AM - Love Language B2B
TimeCop

MONDAY
6AM - Lord of Light's Mt.
Sermon ☼
8AM - Fresh Pots!
10AM - Breadmaker
12PM - John C. Lilly vs
Marcia Moore
2PM - Trevor
4PM - ??? - Beauty Collective B2B

FRIDAY

It has very little to do with the music.

72+ hours of house music, as advertised, but it has almost nothing to do with that.

We arrive early on Friday, park our car, and carry our gear to a primo camping spot overlooking the desert valley we've driven hours to lose ourselves at. All sorts of lessons learned and remembered after years of festivaling, but you damn well better yes sir whatever you say sir show up as early as humanly possible on Friday for it to count for all it's worth. Ugh. Saturday people with their johnny come lately smirks and total disregard for group dynamics and traffic flow patterns. It's equally non-ideal to be a Thursdayer, so caked in dirt by Sunday that it seems like a 26.2 when you've only ever hit the treadmill for 4.

Fridays set you accustomed to the lay of the land like the minuscule pirate map they put on social media 48hrs before liftoff is any sort of accurate representation to the real real estate feet will travel over the course of the weekend, resulting in a palpable lived-in knowledge of where all of the best places to pee are when inevitably tripping balls. This is important.

One fell swoop and I flip my camping chair out to full shape, resting its four cloven hooves down into the dirt next to the cooler full of various alcoholic beverages. A sticker on the top panel reads IF IT'S TOO LOUD YOU'RE TOO OLD. The ice-cold metal of one of the more refreshing options hits my lips, sucking back bubbles like a perpetual oyster machine.

Micah places his chair next to mine, underneath the shade cloth we've fashioned out of years of accumulated tapestries for fear of the big hot ball of gas that threatens to harsh our mellow if allowed too much direct interaction with our traditionally indoor skin. He pops in head phones and throws an eye mask over the portion of the face said mask was designed for, kicking back, while I turn to page 172 of a book that I brought to look smart, but didn't really intend to read.

The space fills in around us, but that's okay because in the insulation power move of the century: these are Friday people. The heads are out in full force and we'll all know where to piss and shit soon enough—that's a guarantee.

A few scattered trees and patches of grass provide some natural shade and carpeting. This is sacred land. Native American reservation, yes, but not that kind of sacred. The kind where you don't talk about the job you've got to return to, or the lack of one. Ex-girlfriends and boyfriends and family issues off the table. Overdue bills and unemployment nixed into oblivion. Really, any and all hostile conversation that could be ordered to go from the seemingly innocuous but notoriously poisonous platitude: "how have you been?" is reserved for about fifteen miles out of town, left at the last minimart gas station before pavement turns to dirt with the $15 you definitely spent on ice.

Old friends and new ones, catching up wasn't a priority, but a mark that you weren't following the credo—"Be Here Now." Ram Dass, 1971. Of course, being centered was easier said than done. We all tried despite. That was what we were here for after all. That *IS* what it had to do with. Drugs helped. Psychedelic consciousness.

As if we'd spoken them into existence, a fairy queen who introduces herself as Vica offers us mushroom chocolates that she made herself. *The chocolate or the mushrooms?*, I don't ask. She tells us the second part before the first, with Micah raising the sleep mask up to his forehead like an incredulous set of eyebrows.

"How much?" I ask instead, more inquisitive than actually interested.
"$10," she responds. "They're about half a gram per."

We look to each other, deciding incommunicado if we'd like to trip on mushrooms or not. Committing to half a gram—or even half a half a gram if we were to split it—of psilocybin on day one was a mistake I'd made before and wasn't about to make again. I remember walking around the forest three miles away from our campground begging raccoons for their mercy. They showed none and I shivered under shrubbery until morning, when by the light of day I was easier to find. Sure I could buy now, imbibe later, but chocolate melts under the hot hot heat and I'm not trying to lick choc off my fingers to make it worth the present me wanting it later. Future me thanks present me for not sucking. Shrooms never come when I want them.

I tell her all of this, and she nods knowingly like gotta make a buck, but I get it buckaroo. She rises from her sales pitch squat, and starts to head off on her way, back to wheeling and dealing, when I tell her to come back later in the weekend and we'll buy a couple, knowing that her returning was about as likely as me still wanting them: an even 50/50. Micah and I wave goodbye to Vica, repeating her name to each other in order to remember it. Vica, Vica, Vica hoping we don't forget it when and if we inevitably want what she's offering. Vica.

With book folded, sleep mask off, and sun breaking behind the horizon line, I lift ass off chair and put myself to work, unfolding tent rods, slipping them into sheaths and raising a piece of camping architecture up and secure. Micah follows suit and soon we're back in the seats admiring our separate bedrooms and/or homes for the weekend. Mine is an orange spaceship that can fit about three people maximum, cross-legged and intimate. Micah's can pop itself up, resulting in more square footage, sure, but Micah is a good half a foot taller than me and claims he needs the extra space to be able to put on pants.

The sky is blue like it always is, but in the freedom of this very moment it's maybe bluer than ever before. The bluest. Looking into the ocean on a clear day, but up instead of down. I mention this to my friend, the one I drove all the way from San Diego with, and he agrees, staring up and sharing in this moment. It's simple, but pleasures often are. It's a nice reminder that we're alive and can have a moment with nature before the storm ain't calm no more.

They—who is they? the unknowable they—say that energy attracts. Equal and opposite. Keep a smile on your face and the good will buzz your way with a smile that puts yours to shame and a perspective that will rock the core foundation of your being into another realm of understanding. All we're able to do is live in our own skin, our own bubble. Empathy is a myth. And though I can't ever truly feel what another does, I can for a brief moment fit myself into their brain and try and see how it works. The dressing room for the mind. Oh, you handle this that way. What I handle poorly, another takes in stride. It's impressive if you're paying attention. I think at a place like this, we're all vibrating at such high frequencies that bumping into someone you're likely to like is beyond probable, calculated statisticians would even call it a guarantee.

Micah and I met at one such event. With the shared communion of friends of friends. My friends + his friends = we friends. It's a simple transitive property. Karate kicks and shared silences are the most I could ever ask for in a friendship. It's all about liking being alone with yourself. If you don't mind the synapses firing and thoughts bubbling to the surface, then it's easy to not prattle on and on about nothing because anxiety is weighing down the button in the brain that says "Talk! Talk about anything so being alone doesn't hurt so bad."

The catch is conversation doesn't solve anything. Sure, sometimes it does. There are instances where a good old-fashioned heart to heart could solve global warming, melt down all the nukes and bring back everyone you've ever loved. But most of the time it's just desperation rearing its ugly head. Micah's not like that. He's perfectly content staring off into nothingness, smiling to himself about the majesty of every moment. This is what I look for in people.

A dude and his lady camped ten yards away from us, behind Micah's monstrosity of a tent, bicker in that playful way that only they think is cute. The rest of the world just wants them to break up and get it over with before they lead a life of misery triggered by passive aggressive behavior. When they walk our

11

way, Micah and I instinctively stiffen up, begging the gods of energy to let this moment pass unscathed. They keep going and I breathe a sigh of relief. Your vibe attracts your tribe. I think they have that printed on t-shirts at Target.

We've both been here once before, but not together. Micah drove up last year, and I a couple of years before that. At a very different place in my life, but here we are again. Between then and now we'd both visited many like-minded places. A good music festival, hell a bad one, exactly like the people within it, has its own kind of vibe. Maybe it's the people who attend, or maybe it's the living breathing organism that went and organized itself into some kind of circus show.

Corporations are people now, right? Have been since 2010. Does that mean other things can be people as well? Can, say, a music festival be personified? If so, then I believe the energy comes from the source and not those who buy tickets and take the ride so to say. Not mutually exclusive either, as one can quite easily be ruined by the other.

6PM is when the music is set to start getting good and I check the time with an eerie precision that tells me in another life I'd make a killing telling fortunes. "I'm going to take a stroll," I tell Micah, who flips me the shaka in return. The shaka, also known as 'the hang loose,' is a hand-sign consisting of an extended thumb and pinky finger so as to express approval. It is popular amongst California surfers, of which we are the first, but not the second. I stretch my tight black jeans across the knee as I rise from my polyester throne bought for $19.99 at Dicks Sporting Goods a year or two before, using a coupon.

Weaving through tents is a pastime of mine, and I'm particularly good at it in this semi sober state. Put the wrong cocktail in me and I might be stumbling through like a fool, knocking over chairs and spilling drinks like a professional football player on the brink of CTE. But not now. Now I slip with finesse.

When it's still light, albeit dwindling, is the time to take spatial inventory, I realize, pausing for the briefest moment to take a mental picture of our set up: it's quaint, chimney in the corner and throw carpet in the foyer, cabanas out round by the pool. When really our two tents underneath a gray EZ-Up looks exactly like every other combination put together.

Hmm, I think, scratching my chin like I haven't shaved in weeks (I haven't) … what to make my little slice of slumber seem different? A light up product would be ideal. LED, Neon, anything to guide against the visual of darkness. This, the sun reminds me, laughing as it sinks lower and lower behind the tree line soon to disappear and leave me with the frame but not the reference.

Slip off to the road and in the same general longitude (I think that's the sideways one, but if the sun isn't that way, maybe I'm on a North-South axis and we should be talking latitude—WHO CARES) is a flag of Do from Heaven's Gate. Instantly recognizable photograph, his hands up next to his head, a surprised look on his face, lecturing his followers about chopping their dicks and pussies off for the Lord or something. Praise Hale Bopp. The flag rests on a short metal flagpole next to the kind of canvas party tent you'd see at base camp in the African Savannah. Long, easily 30 feet and right on the main path. I look around, get an eyeline of Micah futzing around our campsite. This'll have to be my landmark for safe passage home.

I pass more interesting looking people than I could ever appropriately remember. Some wear wigs, scarves, psychedelic pants, no shirt, body paint, glitter, a squirrel suit, a dress made entirely of fake teeth, suspenders, ski attire, formal wear, a see through shirt, clown pants, flower patterns, and entirely neon outfits every which way but loose. For more on hippie fashion please reference Cardin Jordan's *Guide to the Dashiki, and Other Appropriated Fashion Choices.*

We've got short hair, long hair, gender fluidity, people with bicycles for arms, one guy with his face upside down, a variety of races that would make the entire UN give their approval in thumbs up form. Yeah, baby. Each and every one of these beautiful souls (most on the outside, most—but less—on the inside) having the time of their lives, doing whatever they fucking want to.

Drink, smoke, snort, fuck, howl at the moon before it has even come out, jump up and down, run around in circles, giggle with abandon, cut loose, have a good time, be the person they want to be. Be all that you can be. Wait, no, wrong catchphrase. It's a magical thing, really.

Camp [??/\??]—labelled exactly so on a hand painted wooden sign outside their meticulously set up area—offers me a hit from their bright green six-foot bong named Lyle. Lyle has two googly eyes approximately two/thirds the way up the neck, insinuating by placement that the entire chamber from which the smoke has to linger for a comically long time is Lyle's oversized head, with the bowl/carb bubble at the bottom of his miniscule little body.

Though I enjoy this character come to life quite a bit, I turn them down with a smile and a friendly "maybe later." Not the world's biggest fan of smoking weed. Not even in the top 100.

I can imagine this detail to be confounding to those who haven't spent the entirety of their twenties experimenting with drugs, tents, and music, so I feel the need to clarify. I like to get high, but not stoned. Simple as that, wash it away with vinegar and bleach because we're done here, folks. There's an anxiety involved in the consumption of marihuana that many chalk up to just part of the paranoiac experience of being stoned. Try Indica they say, and I'm stuck to the couch like a self-inflicted Spider-Man, plain dumb that would make a redneck seem professorial.

I don't like it. To me, weed might just be the hardest drug in the repertoire. It makes me feel like nobody likes me and everything I do is wrong. I only keep it on the not do-not-fly list because there's a time and a place, a set and a setting.

Molly, Ecstasy, LSD, Cocaine, Ketamine, Shrooms—none of these hold a shade of a whale fat candle to the panic attack powers of pot. I am, what I'd like to consider at least, the best version of myself on almost all of these substances, and especially on egregious combinations of the aforementioned. But baked and I'm a mindless goon, brain shutting down like HAL at the end of *2001*. I like my mind. It's fun to keep around. Why would I try and shut it down?

But marijuana is legal now, they say, Grandma does it every night before she goes to bed. Well power to Grandma that it doesn't stupefy her brain into jelly. I understand the practical medical advances and I see many of my friends thriving, nay prospering, under a daily regimen that could only be described as stoneriffic. Micah will likely end up here at some point over the weekend, smoking enough for the both of us, sucking on the top of Lyle's long head as if in some sort of Herculean effort to rid the world of smoke.

If it's not about the music, then what is it about? I'm not really sure. Compulsion? Habit? Sense of community? It used to be about something, that I know for sure. Growing into the person I am today, experimenting with sex and drugs, escaping from the stress of work and women and waiting for something better with a little R&R (raving & raving, obviously), and hell, sometimes, yeah, even music. I tried my hand at DJing and it didn't really stick. Now I'm just an active participant. There's something about going grocery shopping for five days in the desert that feels more worthwhile than the everyday average run-of-the-mill sustenance providing trip. Like this was for the real me and the rest were just filler. Even if the excitement had waned over time, it felt better than not.

Eight years ago I was brought to my first rave. It was a stage in my life where I was saying yes to things and it was a thing that I said yes to. The friend I went with, let's call her Kayla, even though that's definitely not her real name, doled me out two ecstasy pills a day, and advised me when to take them for maximum effectiveness at proper party o'clock.

I've been stuck in my head for so long, as evidenced through this text, that I never really figured out how to cut loose. Pokeballs helped. Two yellow pressed pills no bigger than a pencil eraser with the logo of a popular cartoon embossed on the face.

The ride, the whirl, the energy, I was bouncing off walls hooting and hollering in the way that only people who've abandoned abandon are able. If this was what fun was I wanted more of it. Time grew on, and so did I, finding myself at more

16

events, massives, raves, festivals than is worth mentioning here, but can be found in total on my Wikipedia page.

Roland Becker
From Wikipedia, the free encyclopedia

Roland Justin Becker (born July 2, 1988), is a misguided millennial with very little to show for his middle-class upbringing and relatively respectable college education. He's tried his hand at every known artistic endeavor to date to mixed results. At **Boston University** Roland majored in the Interdisciplinary field, which was something he had to petition the University for as a result of his lack of focus and foresight.

After a stint in the two major West Coast cities, San Francisco and Los Angeles specifically Roland ended up in San Diego where he discovered drugs and music festivals. He has worked as a house painter, janitor, **Uber** driver, video store clerk, pizza chef, blogger, visual artist, social media coordinator, and production assistant. He currently commutes forty-five minutes each way to a job in an area of town he could never afford to live.
He is single.

Contents
1 Career
2 Personal life
3 Failed artistic endeavors
4 Music Festivalography

When I came to Festivalia 5 years ago, it was in its infancy. The speakers and sound were primo, but there wasn't the kind of infrastructure I'd been used to at the corporate megaliths disguised as underground functions. Art installations, paid performers, stages with individualized names and personalities and lighting setups were the rage du jour. If the stage wasn't better designed and didn't have more than the last one, then what was the point? Bigger was everything.

Until the world caught on and the underground became the only safe haven again. There was certainly a time had at Festivalia, but one worth repeating? I suspected so but ended up unable to convince my friends to come back with me. They said that the music sounded generic. I said it didn't matter.

§

The Beauty Collective, four DJs out of somewhere in Southern California—though I suspect Santa Barbara or North County based on the unlimited money they seem to have to fund this kind of endeavor—were fast becoming the hottest selectors in the scene.

There's four of them. Love Language, TimeCop, Paul McCartney II, and Trevor. They play psychedelic house music, which is really just tech house with a sunny California flair. Imagine the vibe the Beach Boys would curate if they got booked to play a techno warehouse in the UK.

Love Language is the leader of the pack, and by far the most successful. He has tracks released on major labels and the kind of PR that only money can buy. He's got a trademark grin from ear to ear that simultaneously makes him feel down to earth and the world's most intimidating celebrity. This guy could be a model if he wasn't "changing the way the world communicates" (his words).

His older brother **TimeCop** plays dark and moody techno. The sort that is normally relegated to side rooms, or underground basements and never-fails to be between the hours of 3 and 4 in the morning. His mix series is called Witching Hours and you can listen to all 220 hours he's curated on Soundcloud.

19

Those who know more than me have claimed TimeCop to be the heart and soul of Festivalia.

Paul McCartney II is the reincarnation of Paul McCartney, though nobody seems to have the heart to tell him that McCartney is still alive and has been for all of II's 52 years on Earth. Best I can suss out on this one is that it's like some sort of image reincarnation spurned out of the temple of self-discovery. Either way, it's definitely charming enough to not let it get bogged down by details.

And then there's **Trevor**. He's everybody's favorite. Has the best tunes by a margin and a half.

I don't know any of them personally, but through numerous shared experiences, it sort of feels like I'm part of the gang. This is their charm. A feeling of inclusiveness separates the Beauty Collective from the hundreds of other groups of homies playing house music.

I do know Hampton though, and was looking for him.

Hampton lives in a van. That van was likely parked in 'artist camping.' While not entirely a realistic designation considering the come-all come-merry come-wherever credo of the party, the Beauty Collective and their other 40 or so DJ friends tended to be quadranted off in their own little idyllic corner of the map. There were, of course, more trees for better shade, and the kind of luxuries that only come with serious clout and cash. RVs, trailer hitches, shiftpods, domes, lotus belle tents. This was real American glamping. Glamping of course being a portmanteau of glamorous and camping that the Pinterest crowd loves to scroll about.

Hampton was a Thursday person. That's what it took to get the primo spot amongst the elites. That and selling them all ketamine. Hampton was really good at selling ketamine.

Not like that was a thing.

They say don't get high on your own supply, but it didn't really work like that with K. This was a drug that you only sold if you liked to do it. Otherwise, it wasn't really worth your time. He always told me that he'd sell just enough to get his personal stash for free. In my head I always took this as a hint that he was fucking me on the price, but I had cultivated the relationship for long enough that he lowered the price from $100 a gram to $75. I couldn't really complain. Maybe I was being ripped off in the end, but I guess that's dealer prerogative.

Hampton's home is a Mercedes-Benz Sprinter so decked out in special features it was like a luxury condo found wheels and fell out of the sky. With a shine that always looks like it has been freshly waxed, I scoff at what is undoubtedly nicer than my own one-bedroom apartment.

I rap a tap tap on the driver-side window of what I'm sure is his domicile due to the plethora of Grateful Dead and Beauty Collective stickers on the back window.

The door slides open to reveal the scowling face of a woman I've never seen before. She wears dreadlocks, a small bikini and not much else. Fun fact: in all the years I've known Hampton I've never seen him with the same girl twice.

"Hampton!" she shouts back into the van like it's some cavernous mansion and not 200 sq. feet at best. Hampton, mid-toke, looks up from the bong in his hands. His unkempt beard and shaggy red hair shake as he coughs the smoke out of his lungs. The girl in the bikini drops back to her leather seat and returns to painting her nails. At a glance they look like beachside vistas, fit with miniature palm trees and sandscapes.

"Come on in, my man." Hampton says, patting the bed next to him. I take a step up into the single room and shimmy my way between the man and his lady. "Shut the door, why dontcha? Get comfortable," he adds in a way that doesn't feel patronizing in a do-you-think-we-live-in-a-barn kind of way.

I reach over, grab the handle, and try to pull, but the automatic door shut function takes over for me, and we have a herky jerky tango while the robotics get the better of me.

"Bong?" Hampton offers.
"Nah."
"Forgot." Hampton laughs to himself, adding to the girl who couldn't care less about me: "Roland doesn't smoke pot. Can you believe that, babe? Only guy I know who doesn't get baked."
"I smoke sometimes," I say, finding myself defending something I don't really feel the need to defend, but the ego is a strange bird. Dodo. Extinct if you let it get the best of you.

"Weird," she eventually contributes to the conversation, in an impressively disinterested tone.
"Babe, this is Roland. Roland, this is Babe. That's really her name too. I seen the driver's license."
"Did you change it?" I ask.
"Yeah. When I was twelve and got emancipated from my parents."
"Oh shit." Hampton literally can't believe it. "I didn't know that."

"You didn't ask."

It's nice that the conversation doesn't turn to small. We don't discuss how Hampton and I met through my ex-girlfriend. He doesn't ask how she's doing or why she isn't here. He can read the room. Can tell I'm a man on a solo mission and doesn't need to know any more.

Plus, he's not one to talk. Three weeks ago Babe was Chelsea, and in December, I met a girl named Firefly. Instead, Hampton offers me a small bag with white crystal and a miniature spoon that's just the right size for shoveling drugs up your nose and has nothing whatsoever to do with extremely small soup.

"Coke or K?" I ask, even though I don't care which, just want to know what I'm getting into.
"Calvin Klein, baby." Hampton responds. "Designer drugs."

That's cute. Mixed bag. C for Cocaine, K for Ketamine. CK. Calvin Klein. Designer fashion, designer drugs. Surprised I hadn't heard that one before. The mix of cocaine's upper and ketamine's downer is a perfect blend. Hippie peedball that won't kill you. I'm terrible at opening bags, and fumble with the ziploc, feeling around for a place to slip my fingers between.

"Let me help," Hampton offers. I hand the bag to its rightful owner. He places his index finger and thumb on opposite sides, and with a flick of both fingers, the zipper pops open. He places it back in my palm. I dig a spoon in, careful not to get too much and put myself into a hole this early into the game. Ain't trying to foul out before the first quarter even gets heated.

Left nostril sucks up the ground up powder, and I wait for

the drip to hit the back of my throat. Cocaine and ketamine have very different sensations upon entry. Cocaine burns and ketamine feels more like a frog jumping down your nasal passage. I'm able to differentiate between the two and through experienced deduction figure out how high that dose will get me. Not high enough. I ask with my eyes if I can take another and Hampton responds more or less with a pfft of the who even cares bro varietal. I do, switching nostrils and balancing out.

I hand the bag to Hampton and slouch into the surprisingly comfortable furniture. Hampton proceeds to ingest two full spoonfuls of the calvin and/or klein before leaning over me and handing the bag to Babe. She clears her sinuses by pulling the skin of her face taut and sucking up through air. Babe leans her head back as she snorts, pinching the other nostril and pulling harder than is probably necessary. She does this all over again, like a ritual. Clear the sinuses, head back, pinch, pull. I laugh. Hampton laughs. Babe laughs too. The three of us sit in silence save for the intermittent chuckles that bubble up between.

Laughter crescendos and the three of us become a chorus of nothing particularly funny, Flight of the Bumblebees acapella through snorts, chuffs and guffaws. Bumblebee Tuna someone says and the others repeat. Three Ace Venturas in the round. Babe lifts her legs up, stretching into yoga, but a position that doesn't exist, so I guess just stretching. Hampton lies on his back, fingers intertwined behind his head, repeating every Jim Carrey quote he can remember. The man is a walking sound board, alrighty then. I close my eyes and picture popcorn popping. Movie theatre, filling up the frame of vision til I can't see. I shake my head and the popcorn shakes with it, conjuring the space behind my eyes into a snow globe situation. This continues until it doesn't.

Both drugs have a disappointingly short runtime. If acid's 8-10 hours of solid high is a science fiction epic, these are a clip of a cartoon on YouTube that cuts off before the final punchline. We stretch ourselves back into position, normalcy returning to brain and body with a slow-motion snap.

"You got coke for sale too?" I ask, cutting to the chase so I don't overstay my welcome, even though Hampton has explicitly stated that for me the welcome cannot be overstayed.

"150 for the ball."
"Alright, let me get two grams of K, and a ball of coke." I say, reaching for my wallet.
"I'll give you a ball of both for..." He stops to do the math in his head. "350."

In my wallet is fifteen crisp twenties, fresh from the ATM this morning. I can't pull off long division quick enough in the noggin' to figure the price on that, but I know it's a deal and I want it even though I don't have the cash money for it. This feels like a dilemma. I sit there in silence, contemplating how to respond and still get what I want.

"... I only have $300." I say, the cash nearly leaping out of my fingers to get to him.
"Ah, shit. I don't care. Venmo me the rest."

$300 changes hands and fingers press buttons that make apps go, typing in $Hemptown. With a whoosh sound effect like early email servers, $50 is added to the bill thanks to our dear lord Steve Jobs and the Silicon Valley pocket computer that even those of us who have vowed to give up normalcy for 3+

days can't seem to live without.

"Pleasure doing business with you, Roland" he says, dropping two heftily-filled bags on my lap. "This way I didn't have to weigh anything out." I laugh. He does too. Babe joins in. We're echoing our earlier conversation.

There's a moment of silence just long enough for me to take the hint. Slap each hand on my thigh, the universal signal of time to hit the road. I thank them for their time, make niceties with Babe so she remembers me later when I'm just another faceless blob on the dance floor, and come out the way I came in except with pockets full of things I came for, an empty wallet, and a hope that the ATMs are working today.

While this might seem like a lot for little ol' lonesome only me to do these drugs in solitude, the reality is that both are more fun in social settings. Sharing is caring. Sharon is Karen. Anyone who'd rather do their powders on the sly is likely to have a problem. I don't have one. Except maybe poor money management. I do have that. Spending at least $100 that was meant for food isn't what I'd call +++ thumbs up emoji.

Cocaine sucks but is an unfortunate necessity at one of these up all night functions. Plus, once you get a taste you're hooked. Saying this is likely proof to the otherwise in the nature of problematics. Though they say in AA that the first step is admitting that the substance has power over you. Narconon is run by scientology. Crack and smack are whack. I'd like to try PCP. Sometime. Shit that comes out of Big Pharma like Xanax, Adderall and opioids, must be used with extreme caution (as they are habit-forming with an -ly added to the same word used to describe the kind of caution with which they must be utilized (extreme)).

I guess it's all about knowing which drugs drug right for your brain chemistry, and how best to make them drug for and not against you. The girl dancing to greet the sunrise, lucidly talking with her friends vs. the guy passed out face first in a broken camp chair that isn't even his. Dichotomy.

The major distinction here seems to be a simple phrase thrown around at these kinds of functions: "good at drugs." It's a skill that comes easy to some and others will never learn. Follow these guidelines and you should (probably) have a good time.

The landscapes of this kind of festival are always relatively similar. Someone you know you know even if you don't actually know how you know them. Brian? Is their name Brian? You're sure it's Brian. There is a stage or two or three or four or five or six or twelve thirteen fourteen if you're talking European mega-fests and then those are another beast entirely. Glastonbury looks ghastly if you ask me, an American with a slight case of xenophobia. Don't we all?

Here, there is only one stage. Charm, part of the. Unlike every other music festival in the known universe, The Beauty Collective boys say nah. We make the calls, you just live in it. It's sort of like a dictatorship except me and 4,999 others all gladly pay upwards of $300 for the opportunity to be dictated to. Dictated, but not read. It's the little things.

The stage at Festivalia is in the center instead of off to the side or a hike back and forth to camp every time you need to put on another layer in direct relation to the 10 degrees lost per hour from 9PM to 3AM. Brrrr. I wrap my pashmina around my arms just like they do in Kashmir, trying to recollect where our tents were again, but falling on deaf brain cells. Uhhhh. The dance floor will be warm, insulated by people offering body heat and sweating to the oldies.

Where the stage is, center or no, is clear to mine ears, pulling me in the direction of sound. North, South, East, West—SOUND and I'm drawn to it like a cartoon wolf is to a pie resting on granny's windowsill. My legs lift up out of the air and my ears pull the rest of my body along.

Lord lift me up and grant me the serenity of house music, that's all I ask. Nothing more. Give that little boy who can't walk the chance to jitterbug. Tiny Johnny hasn't been able to see since the War and those laser beams are looking mighty fine on this christened eve. The Make a Wish foundation grants Janet Thunderdine her final wish—to see the Beauty Collective crush it one last time. They make good on their no-raving policy that had for years been riling up the community. We watch as the girl is hoisted up on shoulders so she can get a better view. It's a tender moment. We will all attend her funeral in another year and a half, each laying down a tie-dyed rose on top of the shortest little casket any of us has ever seen. But now, she's so fucking high on mescaline that she doesn't even know that there's a floor anymore and the spirit gods long ago taught her about death.

The Map for reference:

```
artistcampartistcamppathinfrastructureparkparkparkparkparkparkparkparkparkparkparkparkparkpa
artistcampartistcamppathinfrastructureparkparkparkparkparkparkparkparkparkparkparkparkparkpa
artistcampHamptonpathinfrastructureparkparkparkparkparkparkparkparkparkparkparkparkparkpa
artistcampartistcamppathinfrastructureparkparkparkparkparkparkparkparkparkparkparkparkparkpa
artistcampartistcamppathpathpathpathpathpathgeneralcampgeneralcampgeneralcampgeneralcamp
artistcampartistcamppathartartartartartartartpathgeneralcampgeneralcampgeneralcampgeneralcamp
artistcampbathroompathartartartartartartartpathgeneralcampgeneralcampgeneralcampgeneralcamp
pathpathpathpathpathpathartartartartartartartpathpathbathroomgeneralcampgeneralcampgeneralge
woodswoodswoodswoodsstagestagestagestagestagepathgeneralcampgeneralcampgeneralcampge
woodswoodswoodswoodsstagestagestagestagestagepathgeneralcampgeneralcampgeneralcampge
woodswoodswoodswoodsstagestagestagestagestagepathgeneralcampgeneralcampgeneralcampge
woodswoodswoodswoodsstagestagestagestagestagepathvendorsgeneralcampgeneralcampgeneral
woodswoodswoodswoodsstagestagestagestagestagepathvendorsgeneralcampgeneralcampgeneral
woodswoodswoodswoodsstagestagestagestagestagepathvendorsgeneralcampgeneralcampgeneral
woodswoodswoodswoodsstagestagestagestagestagepathvendorsgeneralcampgeneralcampgeneral
woodswoodswoodswoodsstagestagestagestagestagepathvendorsgeneralcampgeneralcampgeneral
woodswoodswoodswoodswoodswoodswoodswoodspathFOODFOODFOODpathwoodswoodsw
woodswoodswoodswoodswoodswoodswoodswoodspathFOODFOODFOODpathwoodswoodsw
pathpathpathpathpathpathpathpathpathpathpathpathpathFOODFOODFOODpathwoodswoodsw
generalcampMicah&RolandcampgeneralcampgenepathFOODFOODFOODpathwoodswoodsw
generalcampgeneralcampgeneralcampgenrealcapathworkshops&comedypathbathroomwood
generalcampgeneralcampgeneralcampgeneralcampathpathpathpathpathpathpathpathwoodswoodsw
generalcampgeneralcampgeneralcampgeneralcapathwoodswoodswoodswoodswoodsw
generalcampgeneralcampgeneralcampgebathroompathwoodswoodswoodswoodswoodswoodsw
```

29

The dance floor isn't satisfying. Not with the major case of the shivers I seem to be suffering from. I consider a cup of warmth as the solution to all problems and consult my mental map as to the best way from stagestagestage to **FOODFOODFOOD**.

It takes until about 40 seconds after they hand me a warm cup of coffee, fresh out of the insulated canteen, before I remember the cash I'd brought for this exact occasion has been depleted by my friend and his deal of a lifetime. I curse the fuel in my pocket for the much more reasonable one in my hands, apologizing to the girl behind the counter.

"I'll be right back, right back," I say, with a nervous energy that singles me out as the kind of person who really doesn't belong here, which, if I'm being completely honest with myself, is probably my deepest darkest fear. Oh, the old hip vs. lame paradigm that will haunt those of us who stand somewhere in between for the rest of eternity. I imagine her imagining me in a polo shirt on the weekdays, shudder to think. Time heals all wounds, doesn't it? There's no one else behind me in line, but I set the styrofoam down on the counter and dart to the ATM anyways.

WOULD U LIKE $$$$? The slow-working, anachronistic ATM screams at me. Yes, please, I respond, by inserting my card and plugging in my four-digit PIN. My code represents the date I got the bank card, comfortable sharing this information with anyone because it leaves 365 options, too many to possibly attempt to guess. $160 plus a $3 surcharge hits my bank account and I don't even cringe because money is Monday's problem.

Balancing the checkbook at a music festival seems about the most absurd thing I can think of. Record All Charges or

Credits that Affect Your Account. It's just simple subtraction. Why not? I consider digits while strolling back to Raver Roast (great name I just came up with) at a normal pace. I hand one of the eight twenties to the girl in a sequined smock and swipe my beverage in one fell swoop with the three fives she lays out for me as change.

Why buy coffee when there's cocaine in my pocket? This is a question I ask as I sip the beverage and warm the inside of my stomach lining, tricking my brain into thinking that it's in fact warming my entire body. Not the case and I shiver my way back to the dance floor for exactly 25 seconds before mentally saying fuck this and heading in the direction I think I remember camp being. Worst comes to worst I'll find a new home. Make new friends who'll gladly share my drugs. They'll light a fire by the hearth and let me snuggle down in one of their extra sleeping bags.

My fear is unwarranted as my body's sense of sense memory is more top notch than I give it credit for, and I'm quickly at the Heaven's Gate flag, then Micah, dropping my coffee in a cup holder before teleporting inside my tent and changing into something more weather appropriate.

I say the music isn't what is important, but at a festival built around such a concept, there's almost nothing else, but. So, what's important in the doldrums of buying drugs, drinking coffee and returning back to my tent? Is it the normalcy of it all? This is my life after all. My life between lives. Every day when the days that aren't these don't matter. Hit the reset button. Pick out a long-sleeved layer and pair of pants like it's some kind of major life decision. There is a nothingness here that can only be compared to sitting on the beach in Waikiki. So much to do, unlimited possibilities, like an open-world

Sandbox, Role Playing, video game, where you're piloting your own character. But that character is you. I'm playing a game and I'm playing it well.

Go into the inventory, take out the ketamine. Reach into my backpack, pull out my car keys, and hit that tiny metal square that releases the valet key on the fob. This is perfect for doing drugs with, because it's got a little indentation that can capture and protect powders, as opposed to all the other keys that are just mediocre flat surfaces utilized only in a pinch. We really need to normalize doing drugs in public.

Annnnnd this is the beginning of a story where I lose my car keys and have to spend the next three days trying to find them. A comedy of mishaps where I end up meeting a cartoon character version of myself who, after taking me on a journey through the subconscious mind, makes me understand that I can just imagine the keys back into existence.

The third act has me battling the monster that hid under my bed as a child and the moral of these 230 pages is that I just needed to grow up and get a big-boy job this whole time. Nah. Place the real key inside the backpack safe and sound, ensuring self in the ability to leave when necessary. Close her up nice, I tell myself as I close her up nice.

I do drugs. I do both kinds of drugs. Snoof one up one nost (short, forgot the ril) and the other up the other, then put my thing down, flip it and reverse it. Ti esrever dna ti pilf, nwod gniht ym tup. Ti esrever dna ti pilf, nwod gniht ym tup.

It's good. Drugs are good. I feel like I'm on top of a motherfucking skyscraper, king kong ding dong, but that skyscraper is eternally underwater and even shouting out loud is impossible. Scouring through my clothes becomes some sort of challenge. I don't know what any of these things are or what limbs go in which holes, but I'll play dress-up until something feels right.

The butterfly emerges from his cocoon, with layers secured in sleeves and leg sleeves. Don't know if I look good, but that's what my friend sitting in the chair is for. Micah looks up but doesn't react in any sort of revealing way. Hmmm. How am I to decipher the mystery of the clothed self? Two simultaneous options emerge.

A. I ask. "Hey Micah, old friend, does this look dumb? Am I a fool for being unable to dress myself inside the tent on a dose of drugs ill-advised, but not unrecommended? Most definitely. Is that the answer to this problem? No. The answer is a simple kind-hearted reflection from my fashion-conscious friend. Is this slopped together ensemble a catastrophe or a who-gives-a-shi?" To which Micah would look me over and tell me that I look fine and I'd believe him because that's how friendship works.

B. I look down. The clothes on me are not what I expected, and having to process upside down, my brain requires extra time to decipher if I've chosen wisely or poorly. I scan the shelves of the video store that is my body, inputting each item into an Excel spreadsheet. Pants—check. Black. Not overly gaudy, simple easy decision. Instinct must have seen me through. Up to the shirt and flannel patterns imprint themselves on my vision. Lines and colored rectangles. How standard. How absolutely, upsettingly normal. Pathetic.

"Lose the hat," Micah says, and I reach to the top of my bonnet and pull off a Russian fur hat, straight out of Kiev, slamming back bottles of room temperature VVodka to warm the soul on cold winter nights. "Too warm." He adds, and I can't help but agree. Seriously, I am unable to help myself from agreeing. It's like when he's right, he's right, and this time he's right. Right? In one swift flick of the wrist the hat flies its way into my tent and lands right in my bag. Молодец.

We share in a conversation that doesn't amount to much more than catching up on the familiarities of territory. The more enjoyable part is the cup of coffee. While not so hot it's like what the fuck you trying to kill me anymore, it's still got a bit of heat left in the street.

My throat thanks me kindly good sir, as does my central nervous system, but this neurotransmitter guy starts copping a little attitude, like he's trying to do his job and what gall for me to come in and slam an extra responsibility on his desk. Sorry man, work's gotta get done. Call in the Serotonin reserves. Hut hut, reporting for duty.

Okay, I'm fucking high. When one is high the absolute best move in the book is to get more high. Flick the bags out of my pocket. Fastest gun in the west. Quick Draw McGraw. They both land simultaneously in the palm outstretched like for one fraction of a millisecond I'm a baller motherfucker. Ta-da! I say, ruining the moment for both Micah and I. He rolls his eyes but takes my drugs.

"Which one's coke, which one's k?" he asks, knowing that if I hand him two bags of white powders that one is going to be coke and the other is going to be k. No one does fucking molly anymore. What is this high school?

"Uhhhh" I say verbally instead of inside my head as I bring my eyes closer to better determine the crystals like that's going to make any difference. I laugh. I have no idea. "I have no idea."

Undeterred, Micah takes them both from me. He rests one bag down on his knee and unclasps the other. Around his neck is a silver chain. On the end of that silver chain is a small silver spoon. At the end of his small silver spoon there is a small etching of a frog. The little frog spoon goes into the bag and emerges filled conservatively. Cautious. Just a little scoop. There's no such thing as too much cocaine. I mean, just ask Scarface. But there's definitely the possibility of too much ketamine.

Boom. Floored. In the ground. Tongue lolly-gagging around your mouth and you can't even ask for help, lifted up and outside your body, looking in. Knocking on the back of the skull saying hello dummy wake the fuck up I know you're in there. Body feels it but can't connect to the brain and for a moment it feels like what I've always imagined being a freshly dead ghost would feel like. Am I dead? And then you start to really question it: AM I ACTUALLY FUCKING DEAD? DID I TAKE TOO MUCH?! IS THERE EVEN A TOO MUCH ON KETAMINE? THEY DIDN'T COVER THIS IN DARE. Then someone laughs and says "woah man, Roland took too much. He's in a k-hole." And I've heard of those and my body and soul become one again even if they're not functional. But now, it's like, after years of use, is that even possible anymore? We still spoon cautiously because to be good at drugs is to learn from the lessons that you impart upon yourself.

"This one's Coke." Micah says, as he pulls the spoon away from his nose. He goes back in for round two, knowing full well that if he wants to motivate himself down to the dance floor, he's going to have to do more than the paltry bump he just took as a tester. So he does and then I do. And he does some ketamine and then I do too. It's a game called monkey-see, monkey-do. I'll do drugs with me if you do drugs with you. Bags get passed back and forth, mixed up and thrown down. They both end up back in my hand with no clearer picture of which one is which, or if they even are separate bags at all.

Micah unzips his fanny pack and pulls out a sheet of smiley face stickers. He is a consummate professional, a part-time music librarian with his PhD in—uh—Ethnomusicology, who never talks like an academic because he says it would spoil the fun, though I suspect that the smartest people don't need to speak smart to be smart. I, on the other hand, ready David Byrne's *How Music Works* and regurgitate it almost constantly to appear like I know more about music than I actually do. His—uh—dissertation was on the rise (and rise) of house music, of which the smiley face has been and continues to be a major player. Two eyes and a smile, multicolored, the key art of the nineties acid rave. He peels a purple one off and offers it to me.

"Put it on the ketamine bag," he says.
"Which one's the ketamine bag," I say, pathetically holding them out like a child demonstrating something he found.

"Give them to me," he says. After 3 seconds, tops, of examining them—by eye, don't know HOW he does it—Micah presses the purple smiley face sticker on one of them. He hands it back to me repeating the phrase *Ketamine* so it ingrains in my brain. Purple Ketamine. Purple Ketamine. Purple Ketamine. Dale Carnegie says a person's name is to them the sweetest and most important sound in any language. Say it three times in

36

the first thirty seconds and you won't forget. Purple Ketamine.

Zoom zoom to the dance floor. Can't get too comfortable or we'd never leave.

Loosely limber limbs lounge lavishly. Floating flesh finds functionality as sensations slowly settle into more maximalistic movements. Dancefloor dugouts. Arched backs and pathways through crowds until the speaker sounds. Tribal. The body moves without the mind commanding. Up Down Left Right Start and over again to the beat. Kick drum snare. Boom clap Boom claps. This is what the body was meant to do. Separate. Really resetting. The art of the realm of the invisible, commanding unseen to do thy bidding, pulling the strings but it's okay I told them to.

The DJ on the microphone, or far away and who knows how long ago in a studio on a different microphone, says "to all my muthafuckas…" There's supposed to be more, but it never comes, trailing off as intended, changing only into different music. Sounds that make the body turn and twist in different ways than the sounds before them. I guess I'm one of his muthafuckas my body says, taking the cue and moving along with the song as directed by notes and tones that could probably be scientifically predetermined, but that would take all the fun out of it.

We're hooked in, riding the wave of an ever-changing bassline. The catch is always finding the groove. It's hard when there's people talking in your ear or worries at home, but drugs are anti-anxiety and if done properly all that fades away into this point of Zen where you, the drugs, the DJ, the songs they are playing, and the other people around you coalesce into one. A moving, thinking body, unconscious of the world around them, present in the moment of art. It's nice. So you continue to dance as your way of applauding them for the magic trick well done.

Time is insignificant, and so it passes.

But, yeah sure, whatever, I admit it: the drugs wear off. Not off off naked away ye foul beast, but off, tempered that was nice, but now something else seems nice too. So the distracted brain takes itself on a walk away from one thing and toward another. The spectacular sounds become background and I spin, letting the turn of fate decide to tell me where to go next.

Spin spin sugar round n round, those two songs mash-up as I turn my body methodologically away from the stage, pulling me back in my peripherals with lights and colors meant to keep us entertained. Sneaker Pimps x Ratt (Armand Van Helden's Remix) plays in my head and I stop and land flat on my ass.

Laughing, the seas part and the stars twinkle. Someone to the left of me asks if I'm okay and dude in a leopard print wrestling singlet offers his hand. I pop back up to my feet and dance away like a maniac, singing the song that was in my head. I imagine them shaking their heads and laughing at me.

Find a patch of grass. Lie in that grass. Put my arms behind my head. This is real American relaxing. There are, hold on, let me count them, 2,417 stars in the sky, moving, shaking their tailfeather to the beats being broadcast behind me. I try to single out the constellations I know from the constellation academy. The one with the guy trying to hold up his belt. Big cup, little cup. Fuckin' dogs. It's no use, they're shaking like I was earlier. Before, when I was cold.

A girl takes a seat next to me. Legs behind her back, neck craned down to look at what I'm looking at. She's got long, curly brown hair that scrapes the grass as she contorts into position. She looks to me for an answer, but I don't have one. Nothing more complex than that. Stars. And so I just flat out say it. No big deal.

"Stars," I say, splitting the difference somewhere between defensive and profound.
"Stars," she adds, finally fucking getting it. Like it's the deepest thing in the fucking world, but also way simpler than that.

"May I?" she asks, gesturing to the grass next to me.
"4 sure," I say, making sure to highlight that I said the number 4 and not the word for. This woman exudes gorgeous in a way that makes me sick to the pit of my stomach.

She lifts her head, twists her body and lets that mane fall beside me. We're not at exact the same vantage point, but as far as the stars are concerned we basically are. Two bodies, still, parallel in an expanse of surrounding movement. If the stars were looking back on us they'd focus on 'figures lying parallel' or 'boy meets girl' or 'help, I've fallen and I can't get up.' I don't want to speak first and ruin the moment. My moment turning to our moment could turn quickly to no moment. Thankfully she takes the first stab.

"Did you know that there's a star in the sky for every single

40

star on the Hollywood Walk of Fame?" she asks, as point blank dry as the best shooter in the west. I laugh, because that is not what I expected. She continues on: "Donna Summer. Harmony Korine. Prince."

"I've been thinking about Prince a lot lately," I add, turning away from the stars to look at her.
"What about him?" She stays staring at the stars. I look sheepishly away, down at my feet if my feet were in view.

"That he died of fentanyl."
"Fucked up shit."
"Test your drugs," we say in unison, locking eyes and instantaneously falling in love. Well, I can't read her mind, but mine is going awooga awooga awooga.

I'm an eyes man, and she has them. Two of them. And they're big and they're round and they're symmetrical and they're in her skull. Got a twinkle that makes little stars forget that song about them. Pull out to reveal teeth clamped together and lips pulled back, a sign of comfort that we, people, are able to read on each other's faces. She's laughing. It's infectious. Rats carrying the plague couldn't take out medieval England, but strap this guffaw on some vermin and send 'em out scurrying to get the whole world happy.

"Of course I never do," she adds, looking back up to the night sky shimmering far more impressive than any stage production ever could.

"I even have the tester kit," I say, turning back and away and towards our shared view so as to not keep staring and freak her out, even though my heart is freaking out, pounding in my chest screaming let me out, let me out, I wanna marry this girl.

41

"But I always leave it at home."

She sits up and reaches into her pouch, pulling out a small bag that looks like mine, but has weed leaves printed on one side. She licks her finger, dips it in, and pulls it out covered in dirty white crystals. She pops it in her mouth and sucks it off. Seductive in a way.

"Molly?" she asks. I sit up, pausing through action to consider her proposition.
"I haven't had molly in forever." MDMA, E, Moon Rocks, etc. The drift is gotten.

"Live a little," she says shrugging. She looks like the emoji of the girl shrugging, saying both do it, don't do it, I don't give a fuck, but you probably should all at the same time.

"It's good. It's clean," she adds like that makes any difference and I'm not just going to take it because a cute girl is offering it to me.

So I say fuck it, and lick my finger, dipping it in her finger-sized bag. When my finger emerges it's with much less than she did, but that's how I'd rather it anyways. The chemicals taste just as I remembered. Clorox wipes frozen and chiseled into crystal shards.

The taste hits my tongue and my brain wakes up. Hello old friend, we've been here before, riding that wave of the roll. The brain preps himself for a night out on the town, grabs a sports coat and throws it over the shoulder just in case he ends up somewhere bougie, gucci. "Alright, let's do this," I hear him say as he closes the door to our apartment and struts out into the big wild world.

"Coke? K?" I ask, instinctively reaching into my pockets to reciprocate.

She shakes her head no. "Maybe later." I let my hands hang. She leaps to her feet, extending an arm out to me. "Done looking at stars, star boy?"

I take one last look at the stars, as if that's really even a question with this beautiful face beckoning me, daring me to go with her. Maybe I can't meet a girl in a bar anymore. Maybe no one can, too scared that being forward is the wrong way. Trapped in our phones, unable to initiate. Maybe I've felt deeply lonely since the last girl who started up a conversation at a music festival. Where else can casual chatter just happen? Conversations about nothing—Jerry, Elaine, George and Cosmo. Sitting at the coffee shop reading something provocative, no girl's going to crane her neck over my shoulder and read a line like "mysterious erections" right off the page. Sure, there are conversations to be had everywhere, but I'm not having them, and I don't really know anybody who is.

There is a place, one in most cities, and more than that spread across private lands, desert campgrounds and polo fields, where people touch and engage and put down their phones so that they can live in the real world for a glimmer of time. There is a place where I am charming and wanted, and have the ability to make friends, forge relationships, and actually talk to women. This is why we're here. To be the people our parents told us we could grow up to be.

I grab her hand, and she pulls me vertical, the lights twinkling around her head. It would be nice to ask her name, I think to myself, but that would ruin the mood. Just go have a good time with Noname, I tell myself. Doesn't matter really, but I think I just named her after a rapper I saw play live once.

When she runs toward the dance floor, I follow, trying to keep pace, weaving through groups laid out on tapestries, kicked back and enjoying the music in a casual setting, girls hula-hooping, and people smoking cigarettes outside the immediate circle of influence. How courteous.

"Hey man, Hey!" I hear behind me, a familiar voice that grates up my spine and back down again. "Roland!" Hand rests on my shoulder. Cheese, grate, feta crumpled on a plate of regrets. Pick the one cheese that isn't grated. Great. I turn back to put a face to the holed cowbell of a human being. This royal shitbag's name is Ronald.

Exactly like mine if you invert a couple of letters. He follows me on Instagram, and he thinks we're friends, but we're not friends. This shit might seem all puppy-dog tails and roses, but there's negative aspects too. You can't have 5000 people show up anywhere without a couple dozen scumbags. I especially like the word scumbag when I consider its etymology.

"Oh shit, hi man," I say trying to sound as genuine as I'm able, while really taking the moment to glance back over my shoulder for Noname. She, like her given name, is nowhere in sight, no how waiting for me, no chance at finding her. Lost to the sea of bodies shaking and shimmying between here and infinity.

If we were ever cool once, Ronald and Roland, we aren't anymore. Especially not now, not ever again after now. Read the fucking body language of the people around you, man. Someone rushing through a crowd, it's probably not to talk to you.

We stand there in silence for a moment, while I fume, thinking of everything I hate about this guy. His dumbfuck obsession with sweaters, the way his moustache is longer than the rest of his facial hair, how he regularly posts selfies and hashtags them #selfie, the fact that he's here even though he's always complaining that the Beauty Collective are like a cult or some shit.

"Do you know anybody that's got coke?"

Reaching into my pocket, I grasp that bag like it's his neck and I'm ringing it. Ring a ding ding, chokehold motherfucker, window smashes Austin 3:16 theme loops in the background.

I wake up from my dream state, fake smile plastered across my face. Molly has this great effect where you love everyone deeply, aren't bothered by minor inconveniences and feel all of your emotions tenfold, but when there's no love, it's way hard to fake it. I've got no outpouring of emotion for this guy who's only in my life because we share the letters of a name. It's bullshit. There's no way he's getting any of this coke, nor will I tell him about Hampton. Hampton's my guy. The only people who get his contact info are people who I know are the real deal. Probably end up stiffing him. I can't take that black mark on my rep.

"Yeah, I've been looking too," I say, bold face lying like it's all I know how.

"Oh well yeah, well no big deal. If you find some good shit let me know," he replies like I'm some kind of drug dealer just because I sold him drugs once. You do a favor for people and it bites your ass off sometimes. We stand there again in a shared moment of noiseless avoidance, like all he fucking wanted was me, a guy who knows how to get drugs, to help him, a guy who has no fucking clue. Finally:

"Alright, well I'mma try and find that girl I was following," gesturing to that point in the dance floor where I lost the girl that was probably nothing, or maybe we were going to kiss a little bit, or maybe we'd date for a year and she'd ruin my life—who knows. I hear him say oh wait, but it's too late, I'm already gone, bee-lining through people to get the fuck away.

No Noname, but I do stumble on Babe. Sweat pouring down my face, she doesn't recognize me. As predicted. "It's Roland, Hampton's friend," I yell over the music. "Oh Hampton? He's right over there," she points to the back of an ostentatious fur coat.

I bounce over to my friend, who it turns out is in the middle of a transaction, selling coke to a dude with a beard that would make the guys in ZZ Top jealous. Beardson is shaken by my overabundance of energy, skin melting off my bones, weird on the come up.

"Yeah, yeah." Hampton adds to finish off the sale and get back to his people. "Just holler if you need anything else. I got Deem too if you need it."

The dude nods and disappears into the dance. Hampton turns to me and laughs. "Bitch, you rollin?" he asks. I bite my lip and nod my head.

"Your pupils are bigger than ya nips," he adds, laughing.

"Fuuuuck," I run a hand through my hair, fingers coming out drenched like I just put in product. I hate fucking MDMA and I tell him as much.

"Yeah, yeah. What you need is to smoke some pot. Come with me, let's roll a jay."

For some reason I don't say no. I know it's the right thing, remembering my first twenty or thirty raves before powders or psychedelics where reefer cut the roll and centered the body back towards somewhere that wasn't way the fuck over here. He whistles to Babe and gestures to the back of the dance floor. She acknowledges, but turns back to the DJ, sending us off on a mission for two.

Hampton pops down next to an inflatable elephant double the size of a real one—it's impressive, really, and definitely not the right color: Yellow and Purple Yin Yang—his back resting on the rope that helps tether this balloon creature to the ground. He pats the dirt, offering the spot next to him on the ground. At first I decline saying something lame about how I need to keep dancing right now, but he insists as forcefully as he's able, which is really just suggesting it again with a sense of sage wisdom through the twinkle in his eye.

I pop a squat, unable to fully sit, but this way I'm able to rest on my haunches and sway side to side. My friend, with a rolling paper pressed between his fingers, sprinkles grass in the tube like he's done this once or twice or three times before. With the flick of a wrist, it rolls itself up, rising up to his mouth to lick the paper and seal it shut. Tip to the lip, fire to the other end and he's inhaling, embers burning away paper and plant into oblivion. He hands the joint to me. Reluctance disappears and I take the stick straight into my lungs, inhaling in a sense of fond familiarity.

Lungs communicate to brain and body, both mellowing in a matter of moments. It's the simple things really. Not as complicated as I forget to remember it can be. The smoke twirls its way around my major organs, doing the work the plant is designed to. What's a higher power if not natural solutions to a better world.

I let my ass fall to the ground, legs out in front of me, landing in the grass with a thud. Puff puff pass and my fingers return the joint from whence it came. Thanks man, I say by finally relaxing. There are a million phrases along the lines of told ya so that could come pouring out of his lips, but instead it's just another puff of smoke held in the lungs.

The two of us sit and share, him taking huge rips, and me tiny ones, all too aware of what this substance can do to me if left to its own devices. I love this guy; I really do. We've been through a lot together. Lots of good times. It's been a while, but time doesn't change shit. He puts an arm around me because he feels it too. Yeah. This is nice.

A hush comes over the crowd, the music fading until there's nothing left. A voice comes over the speakers, but it sort of sounds like my high school intercom. Mister Becker, report to the vice principal's office, we've found Schedule III narcotics in your locker and just want to make sure you've got the appropriate prescription for them. What is Rhinoceros grade? Except those aren't the words, and not anything like them either. Maybe it's intonation that triggers me back to once upon a times.

"Hey, hey, everybody. How are you all doing tonight?" the voice asks through the speakers. Or a microphone connected to the speakers. A howl, up and out of the crowd like the wave at a baseball game. It doesn't all start at once, but carries across the field in spurts and bursts. "It's nice to see so many of you made it out for night one this year."

"It's Love Language," echoes through the crowd in near perfect unity with my own brain saying that same thing. Micah slaps me on the arm with the back of his hand and repeats the same thing we all just thought and said. What a strange stirring command he has over us.

Love Language prattles on and drops words like grateful, humbled and excited to the sea of faces squinting to see him, even though we would recognize that voice anywhere and hardly need visual confirmation to know that the man who brought us all here, was in fact up there. His voice ingrained in our heads after a series of songs featuring him talking on the track.

It all started six or seven years ago with a tune called "Commandment" that featured very detailed instructions of how to love thy neighbor. Literally. The song blew up alongside a viral video of an impromptu orgy at the Burn, but by the time it made it out of the dust and into other DJs sets, it had lost some of the sexual depravity along the way. The voice became instantly recognizable amongst a developing stable of the Beauty Collective's hit tunes.

The prototypical example of starting a scene and letting the people follow. First year of Festivalia saw this all begin to coalesce with only 35 paying customers, two CDJs, a mixer, some speakers, and three basic tenants: Art is for Everybody (in Equal Measure), We Like to Party, and Who Cares? (all of which are plastered on hand-painted signs across the festival). Over these past ten years Love Language has grown into the kind of public figure people just seem to want to be friends with. *Mixmag* called him "affable in a way that almost seems alien." He always books artists that haven't broken yet, makes time for his fans, and even started a charity to help kids in underrepresented communities learn how to DJ. Basically a human thumbs up.

"This next act is real special. I don't think many of y'all have had a chance to hear Nys Funk play yet, but I'm sure you'll quickly see why we booked her."

Someone grabs the microphone and screams woo! Love Language continues, undeterred, "Anyway, when's the last time we steered you wrong?"

Collective laugh. Emphasis on collective. It's eerie, goose pimples protruding from my skin, but maybe that's just the combination of MDMA and a slight breeze and not the haunting notion of groupthink. "She's all the way from Guyana, so give her some love my people."

His voice holds on 'people,' dragging it out, as the two to three thousand of us who made it out for the first night of festivities cheer as loud as we possibly can. As if commanded by the God above. The track clicks on with a kick drum that tells the group exactly the rhythm we'll be dancing on. A deep soulful wail follows, leading the way to a funky groove. We finally breathe, the sense of the unknown stressing us out and the release of bass telling us that we weren't wrong in trusting the man who gathered us here today.

2004: Soulwax, a Belgian electro duo, consisting of two brothers: David and Stephen Dewaelae release "E Talking." Or rather the 2005 Nite Versions remix, the one I really remember from my proto days of raving before it all got so complicated and oversaturated. Live long enough in a scene and you'll see it become many things. Nightclubbing to German Acid Techno turns fast all the way to South American funk if you're not

51

paying attention. It's not you, it's the E talking.

Nearly 20 years and I'm remembering the song for the first time in a long time. Long time listener, first time caller, I guess. And while I'm not technically on ecstasy but on MDMA, what's the difference really outside of being cut with a little bit of speed? Either way I'm chattering away in my head about how this might just be one of the best sets I've ever seen, distracted by my thoughts, but moving fully to the music. Too hyper focused in the feel of my body and skin to even look up and watch the DJ do her job. So engrossed in the sound, that for a second I believe in music again. The healing power of turning your mind inside out and setting your body and emotions on right. One tune can save the world, you've just got to get Stevie Wonder and Cyndi Lauper in the recording studio together. This might just be the best music I've ever heard, but it's not me, it's the E talking.

The next 118 minutes pass in seconds, blurring dance moves and beats into a blender hit on max energy whooshing and jumping and sailing around with my people. My people! This is how it's supposed to be. How it was. Take long enough away from molly and she can treat you right. Gonna feel like shit in the morning, but that's the morning's problem. Fuck you morning me. Now, my head's in the clouds, every star shooting and I feel an overwhelming strength of emotion toward everyone around me. Brothers and Sisters from different Mothers and Misters, but that's a cliché, and I hate when I rely on those.

I release high fives like I'm making it rain, or like Oprah giving people merchandise they don't need under their seats. You get a palm, you get a slap, you get hand skin touching hand skin, reaching out, touching me, touching you. Now Everybody—

Moon ain't full, but of shit. I pull myself away from the music. The rest of the world seems so inviting, and after tunes this transcendent whatever starts playing after is not popping the same way as Miss Nys Funk Esquire III. Tracks that feel 14 years behind, stuck in the stone age of tech house. That's what the future'll do to ya. Maybe I just need a breather, overheating around all these people anyways.

Pull at the collar of my shirt as I pull myself out of the crowd and towards a glowing rectangle. It slowly turns from green to blue. Snails pace through the rainbow, but I'm engrossed even at my sped-up rate. This is art? Sure. I stand alone in a portal, shifting between realms and versions of me. Sitting seems ideal, so I do. The light surrounds and I know what it feels like to be Jesus. They strobe in line with the oohs and ahhs of beachside crowds watching a firework show.

Use my phone to check the rest of the schedule to see if/what I need to bother over, though I know I already don't. I'm here because I know I don't. Bothering is for the children.

Know I'd never remember it all but take note of the artists I want to see or had heard were good or just had cool names (Trevor, LL, Paul McCartney, The Beatles(?), T.U.R.B.o., RBCCA, C'est Magnifique, TST). Hopefully bookmarked brain times will stick in there well enough that watch and want would coordinate effort to prioritize time and body into the same plane of existence. If not, that was okay too.

Nys Funk was all I really needed. Walk away with one great set worth more than anything forced or desperate, trying to see it all just to say you did. The glow around me turns from yellow to orange in what feels like a warm embrace of the sun even though it's still hours away. I hate to see the sun come up by

53

myself. Always makes me feel strung out and lonely. Wish I hadn't lost that girl. Felt like we really had something. Maybe. I don't know. What am I projecting?

There's an ultimatum running through my head. Two options, neither of which fill my heart and soul and mind and body with warmth and happiness, but seem like the only viable pathways as the night gets colder and the dark of the night starts to really settle in on itself. Go to bed or don't.

While on paper 'don't' feels like the only option because of the drugs coursing through my system, there are also such things as benzodiazepines to help ease the brain down to nothing and settle me into the sweet embrace of slumber. I know exactly where they are in Micah's tent. This isn't our first rodeo together, and with a prescription that he hardly uses except to come down off drugs, I know I'm welcome to as much as I need.

And there is the real don't, and not the antithesis of it. The one where I snort some powders and make my way back to the dancefloor. Maybe I'll run into the girl, maybe not. Maybe we'll see the sun come up together or maybe Micah and I will, drinking light beers at the campsite. Or maybe a third fourth fifth alternative that I can't begin to realize because the pieces of that puzzle aren't yet in my realm of understanding, the limitless possibilities of adventure branching off into more than I could begin to conjure.

Nah. There's two more nights of this. It's a marathon, not a race.

I drag my ass back to the campsite, familiar with the way now, and grateful to Friday for this simple directionality that will benefit me in the long run. There's a comforting silence at the campsite. Sure the bass thumps behind me, but there's almost nothing else, just the soothing rub of music surrounded by nature.

Unzip Micah's tent, and there in the front left pocket is a small zipper container. Contained within is a miniature pharmacy of drugs that one might buy behind the counter if a psychologist were to believe them when the proper symptoms were described. Benzos, Opiates, Adderall. Not that Micah abuses any of these. You know the habits of your best friends. Drugs are currency here. Show up with what you can get your hands on and it'll come back two-fold.

I break off half a xanny bar instead of my usual quarter because I'm rolling pretty hard and would hate to have to come back for more. Put everything away and zip it all back up. Not trying to pass out in the entryway of another dude's tent.

In my tent, snug in the sleeping bag, the lights of the night flutter across the orange nylon. Lullaby of bass brings me toward sleep. Vision gone, seconds breaking into halftime. Powering down. One last coherent thought before—

FADE TO BLACK

SATURDAY

Serious grog. Eyes feel crusted shut, head pangs, sweating through my clothes. The cadence of the music hasn't changed, but the light sure has. Sun heating up the tent like a pressure cooker. I roll over and try to fall back asleep but awake is inevitable. Pants off, sweatshirt off, fish into the bag for a fresh pair of boxer shorts. Peel the ones I have on off my balls and change into a fresh pair of duds. Might seem much to pack two pairs of underwear a day, but I know what I need to make it through.

Micah sits and I stumble toward him. Shade beckons me like a great protector. Brain can't, and I tell him that. He laughs. Not funny. He offers me a half-smoked joint that I kindly reject with the swat of a wrist that's about as cordial as I can get right now. Ffffffffuuuuuuuccccccckkkkkkk.

A kiss of cocaine to the nose sets me right(er), digging myself out from a Xanax haze that only I can be held responsible for— or is it the molly hangover? Coke doesn't have me rocketing out of my seat juggling sledge hammers, but more of a shot of cold brew straight to the dome on a sleepy Saturday. Wake up!

Maybe I'll take a ride over to the farmers market. Lavender and Strawberry scented cocaine has been the flavor of the month, but I'd pay beaucoup dolores for some coffee flavored coke. Combine uppers into one super upper, lightning shooting through the heart of your soul. Coffee cocaine—too hot of a product for the market, real deal Colombian. DEA agents breaking down doors begging chemists to stop making their drugs smell so damn good. *No can do, sir.* Agents can't help themselves, shoving their own faces in piles of powder screaming hoo-ha, but mixing up their Pacino characters. Say hello to my coffee friend.

Two sniffs for Micah, one in each nostril and he livens up for possibly the first time all weekend. Eyes wider than a Pokémon character on Spring Break in Tijuana seeing their first Donkey show. That moment where they turn from 'what's going to happen' to 'omg what's happening...' You laugh because you've been here before. But this poor defenseless animal warrior has no idea what's coming. Now he's living life on the edge. Says he doesn't even want to move back to America. This is home now. He's got a little shack lined up with a girl named Maria, and they're living the simple life, away from the hustle and bustle. Shook, you leave, hoping that one day you'll see your friend again, but fearing for the worst. Fuck, now I have to find a new Squirtle.

"Thanks, I needed that," he says, handing the bag back to me. Hair of the dog, except a different breed. They say what doesn't kill you makes you stronger and battling a hangover with more drugs is sure to make me Superman. I fly through rings in the sky, battle Lois Lane and save Doomsday. Or is it the other way around.

It's quite simple. Friends share drugs. Pilfering some Xanax from my buddy's stash is the perfect pre-emptive repayment for the plethora of casual bumps Micah will be receiving. There is approximately zero-percent chance this will come back to bite me in the ass. But just saying that out loud shall summon the demons of Chekhov's Gun in reader's minds. Just remember, I'm not like other girls.

I feel around my pockets for the ketamine bag, stickered so graciously by my friend to my left, and clutch it close to my heart. The way one would cling to ground if lost at sea for an extended period of time. So I take a fat bump, one that would be ill-advised for a first-timer, but considering the circumstances, the perfect amount to get me where I need to be.

The trick is riding the line. Right on the edge of the hole, without falling. It takes a second to kick in, and in that last lucid lapse I offer the bag to Micah (he declines) and hop to my feet. A bump that big will have me couch locked if I don't take action and make myself mobile.

The wobbling walk through tents, camps of people drinking and thinking out loud through words—conversation. I hear bits and pieces, but none of it makes any sense. Climb across the mountains: slippery slopes between tents, dodging under ropes without chopping my neck off. Today's not the day to die, but to do, and I'm being a doer. I'm doing.

When I hit the road it's full of people. Beep beep, traffic. Except I'm the drunk driver, swerving in and out of fresh faces. Wrong way down the highway. Clean, smiling, Saturday people. Things are heating up for the weekend. Paul McCartney is on tonight. Of course these people only show up for the name they know. Oh well. More for me.

Strolling in sunshine, minding my business. Trying not to judge. Positive minds breed positive experiences. I don't even know from what really. These new faces could be people that arrived yesterday, but there are *so* many more of them. Like the hustle and bustle of a Medieval town. Simple life. Entertainers, Artists. Merchants selling wares. Get your t-shirts. Commemorative spoons. Pins to put on your hat and stand out for sure as a drug dealer type. Steel-plated boots or nickel-engraved boutonnieres or whatever dumb merchandise grabs the eye. No thank you. Not today, I've got coffee to buy. This is a major mission, but majorly taking the legs off it.

At the end of the hill is a clearing. Check the mental map for reference. Straight is uh where? Right is woods, nothing, edge of the known universe. Close my eyes and let the other four and a half senses take over. I'm only 45% telepathic, but you've got to round up in times like these. Sniff sniff. Nothing. Clear the nasal passages, pulling them apart and sniffing harder to get a whiff of where beans are being roasted.

Instead, those leftover crusties hitching a ride on nose hairs waiting for their chance to attack shoot up into the brain. Kablam. Except the attack is welcome. Not invited, but not unwanted. Like an old college roommate stopping in town for a drink. It's all good even if you end up getting a bit too fucked up. The drip in the back of my throat confirms an increased dosage (so scientific) making its way into my nervous system. Laughing/smiling becomes a way of life instead of just second nature. Whistle if I knew how. What am I doing?

Confused faces spin around me, people wondering where the bathrooms are. A nod, a wave, a 'woah, he's having a good time,' said with partial judgment but mostly jealousy. I ain't fazed because you can't be judged by what you don't mind and yes I am in fact having a good time.

59

The map pops in my head. So I swivel, physically intentional, overshooting by 90 degrees and coming face to face with a frightened girl who leaps back with a little shriek that's simultaneously cute and sobering.

"Happy Festivalia," she says, a bit timidly, but also earnestly and excitedly and also ly.

"Happy Festivalia!" I respond, words floating out of my mouth completely skipping past that part of the cortex that would say that ain't right. Butterflies and bumblebees. She laughs (scared? amused? both?) and continues on her way, side-stepping to get around the man nearly twice her size blocking her path. And I, in turn, continue on in mine.

One cup of coffee please, I say, extending a five-dollar bill, hoping it's enough, and not really caring much if it isn't. Hot or Iced? So I shoot my shot and answer the girl (same from yesterday? Shit, I don't remember, but she doesn't seem to recognize me either, so we just continue playing this game of blissful ignorance except this time I take note of a nose ring, braids pulled back, and fifteen to twenty thousand bracelets as she takes the five dollar bill from me and gives me $1 in return. I drop that shit in the tip bucket and wonder how the hell I'm going to get myself out of these parentheses? I leap, pushing thr)ough the rounded edge and land back on the other side of the transaction, iced, walking away with a chilled batch of beverage, sucking straw and shooting salvation straight to the mind's eye saying wake up in a way that normally cocaine can only do. A fleeting feeling unmatched by the reliability of known quantities. Ahhh that's brisk, baby.

Food: It's not super important when on a diet of powders, but I take a glance at my options to see what I'm dealing with when those inevitable pangs stab painfully as if to say you're empty bruh, give me some kind of gnarly wave to nosh on. Take inventory of three of the six options (falafel, rice bowls, burger) and I'm instantly bored. Like who cares even? Who is this for? Am I going to ramble on about cheeseburger toppings for a page and a half? Cheese and sauce dripping off grilled cow meat like that serves any significance but a later endeavor. A major plot point when I turn vegan.

Brain, remember there is food and that it is here. Specifics are for suckers and I'm no sucker. The foodies drooling at the potentiality of this paragraph like it matters and they can actually try some of this hippie gourmand shit. Pssh.

With the drugs starting to temper their hold, still working but not like WorKkinGg if the drift is catchable (*WOooOOORkinnnnnnnGGGGgg*), I look for somewhere to keep this ride riding. Between two of the food booths sits a small stage I'd never taken the time to notice before. [Like I'd been looking]. Only about thigh-high and much less of a whole rigmarole than the main stage. On it stands a man with a silver goatee and the clothes of a pirate, combining words into sentences.

"We're all just figments of our own imagination. I mean, I know I exist, but that's because there's this thing in my brain telling me that I do. But what if I don't?"

I hold my hands out in front of my face, sending messages between the fingertips and the frontal lobe. I look for a confirmation, but don't receive one. He continues on.

"What if this were liberating instead of terrifying?" My attitude shifts with this question, and I peer past my fingers to the goateed-sentence man who has begun strumming a harp in rhythmed cadence with his speech. I've never tried public speaking, but I don't think I'd like to. That's a lie, everybody has to do it at least once in college. I was fine at it.

I move closer to the short side stage with my attention fairly rapt. "Maybe we aren't real. Maybe we're all just conjured up by imagination. That the atoms we think hold these corporeal ape sacks together are just freeform floating, dreaming this solidity—" he slaps his skin, flesh pounding under the pressure "—into existence."

He pauses. Maybe we share a moment of eye contact or maybe we don't. Maybe there's someone else behind me who actually locks eyes with Dr. Mongoose (is that his real name? How do I know that? Why am I so sure of it?), but I pretend like it's for me. That we share this moment, breathe in, breathe out, consider. I sit. He continues.

"Everybody close their eyes." I close mine. Closesesest they've ever been. I imagine dolloping hot glue on the lashes so they'll never open again. "Breathe with me."

He breathes in a staccato that sounds an awful lot like the *Looney Tunes* theme song, and while that might seem distracting, it centers me, because it's something I know and can participate in.

"Big breaths. Hit the highs, hit the lows. Small little big breaths. Fast. Get out the bad energy. Get out the part of you that says I refuse to believe. I am a person. I matter. I am not a person. I don't matter. I don't mind. I am only a mind. A small little piece of you is still holding on, breathe it out. Big fast breaths. Let it go. Be one with the consciousness."

I'm trying, I really am. Breathing fast and erratic, out, shooting the negative energies out of me. The stuff that says I'm not good enough or I don't belong here. That I'm different because I'm anxious, trapped in my head, trapped on the page, that maybe I'm just being conjured up word by word, detail by detail in this void that we all collectively belong to.

Sure, I can buy this. It's nonsense, but we've all tried LSD before. We understand cosmic karma, the joke. The fucking hilarity of thinking we can control things outside of our immediate control. Why not just go one step further? Take the leap into not existing at all.

Just as I'm about to dive off the diving board of life he pulls us back in with a "Hey now wait a minute." Breaths hold in unison. "That might be scary to some, Dr. Mongoose. That might be taking things just an inch too far." Did he—? We exhale, balloons shooting into the sky never to be found again. "There's something in the middle, maybe?" he asks, but not like really asking, though I'm sure there was a question mark at the end of that statement. Imagine the image floating through my brain.

"If this is all part of our imagination and we don't *really* 'exist.'" He does the air quotes. "Then shouldn't we be more in control of where things take us? Shouldn't we be able to conjure magic for ourselves? Get what we want, when we want it, and how we want it?" We all laugh. I've become one with the cellular compounds next to around behind and beside me. We listen and move and think in the comfort of oneness.

"I guess what I'm saying… is maybe we already are." People move into the thinker pose. The famous sculpture with that dude who's got his hand on his chin as if to say 'I'm thinking here.' "We're here after all aren't we?"

It connects. Ball to bat, slow motion out of the ballpark. Synapses firing in each of us shocking us awake from the slumber that is perpetually dormant inside. The part who forgets how to be and do and see and lives on a borrowed supposed to, checked out of the library for seven days and maybe even hinging on a late fee.

"We each made the choice to be here. To take in this beautiful wonderful weekend full of beautiful wonderful people together. What is conjuring imagination but making choices? You made a choice for your being, and now the being is better off for it. Wow. That's a big one. Say it with me."

"Wow."

And he pauses longer than the first time. This goes on forever, but like a forever that's an exaggeration of about a minute. "Now, just do that more often. Make choices that reflect the imaginary being you want to be. Wish good things upon yourself and good things will come upon you. The only thing holding us back from the reality we desire is ourselves."

He stops strumming. A moment that sends shockwaves through the crowd. He picks it back up, leading where he left off. "So maybe being imaginary ain't so bad, huh? If we act imaginary, then we are imaginary. And if we are imaginary then we can go out and gosh darn mister falcon yippee yi yo ki yay make the best lives for ourselves."

The music stops again. He slowly rises to his feet and takes a bow as we applaud with gusto. I applaud the loudest because I feel deeply connected to this idea, and I want my hands to be heard the most loudly. I even hoot/holler. The speaker grabs the microphone and thanks us all. He re-introduces himself as Dr. Mongoose—no idea how this came to me, that telepathy thing might have more truth than fiction—and asks us all to please make sure to come to Lord of Light's Mt. Sermon (his mainstage set at 6AM on Monday Morning or Sunday Night). He repeats it.

Dr. Mongoose stands at the edge of the stage as an MC rambles on about how the next workshop is for making your own soap, listing off the credentials of this soap-maker extraordinaire. I approach the hero of my day, but he stands chatting with two young girls that seem deeply infatuated with him. I slink away, slurping coffee through straw and trying to piece together why I feel so goddamn victorious after listening to that man speak.

ᔆ

I consider my existence. Which is really quite a hilarious thing to do if you think about it. Metametacognition. Thinking about thinking about thinking. How often does this happen outside of moments pushed to the edge? About to die in a hospital bed. Or holding onto a rope and a couple carabiners, thousands of feet above what could once be considered ground. Or in a classroom where our brains are being taxed with material unfamiliar. As far out as it gets, man. Pressed outside our comfort zone and asked to think about something new. To consider not only our existence, but that of those around us.

And maybe that's what drugs are? Sitting on the edge of our personalities, looking back with perspective to a point where we're more suited to fully realizing ourselves. Funny stuff. Thinking about thinking. But seriously folks, Jay Leno. Progress. Forward momentum. It's not every day that the brain is shook alive, wake up there are things around you that go unseen. The perpetual smile on the grocery bagger's face or the color that shimmers off an office building downtown. Why aren't we always paying attention? It's hard. But THIS (this being Festivalia, drugs, community, music, the combination of forces) makes sure we see. So we think about thinking because otherwise we never will. Will just keep going 24/7 until we die without a single thought ever entering into our brains.

Am I real? Of course I'm real. Physical hand touches grass, pulling leaves of green apart with intentional pressure. Two forces, one exert one inert, creating a reaction, rippling back to position. What's more real than that?

Of course, this is a silly conversation. But the fact that we're having it—we: me and me, the you I constantly reference, the self removed, the ego on hiatus, vacation Roland, a catalogue to carry when all of this is said and done—is the important thing. The takeaway, the point, the joke, the lesson, I could go on and on (Justice - "On'n'on" 2011).

Dr. Mongoose was up there trying to shatter realities, and maybe he succeeded. But mine, is piecing itself back together, freshly reminded of all the reasons I've been brought here. I sit in silence a moment, trying to find a capstone to this thread: a paragraph that surmises and summarizes into the kind of phrase that's found underlined in pen in used paperbacks.

Imagination is the only control we have, because without it, we're stuck believing that good enough is, when it definitely isn't. There's so much out there asking for our dumb fucking eyes to look at it, and if we're too busy worrying about what our hair looks like, we're never gonna see anything outside of ourselves. Take the self out of the equation and there's a lot fucking going on.

Except I realize I've been sitting in the middle of a busy thoroughfare without any regard for the others around me. I look up and out, eyes connecting with flesh and color and auras and it's dope and I shake my head awake as I rise to my feet. Remove thyself from thy self.

Roland's eyes blink twice as he spins slowly in a circle,

catching glimpses of—

Wait, wait what the hell do I think I'm doing? If I'm going to third-person disassociate, I'm at least going to do it on my own terms. The out of body experience is right at my fingertips, literally twiddling between index and middle, back and forth, back and forth. So I turn my body, instinctually, toward the row of blue boxes where piss and shit happens.

There are people standing around, but they are all far enough back that it reads to me as boyfriends waiting for girlfriends and groups chilling on the sideline for the one lone bathroom user. Nobody is there to use these as intended. I guess neither am I. I slink right up to the front and trail alongside the bathrooms until I hit one with a green OPEN sign next to its handle that doesn't reek so bad that my stomach says nah. I find my target, flip open the door and close it latched shut behind me.

Not a pretty sight, festival porta potty. You're guaranteed to get a waft of somebody's physical expulsions out of that sunken hole of blue water. Like blue masks the scent completely. Nah it's a mask that you can still totally see a person's eyes through. Duh we know who you are. To know Bruce Wayne intimately, would be to know he's Batman on first glance. The same thing except with the festival bathroom and the smell of shit.

I don't have time to describe all five senses—and trust me, each one's bad—because I want to get in and out and back on with the rest of my life. The least amount of time in one of these as possible, and pray pray pray that they're freshly cleaned when it's time to do my own actual business.

Daylight hour drug use is a whole different ball game (see:

baseball vs tennis) than night time. Standing around shoving spoons up your nose for the whole world to see feels… ill advised. Even at a place as young, wild and free as Festivalia. Maybe even more so. Let the guard down just enough, but not all the way. That's how trouble happens. That is bad at drugs.

Spoon. Nose. Sniff.
Spoon-Nose-Sniff
Clasp the bag shut.

I notice the fluttering of white particles that fall out and onto my shirt. Pick them up instead of brushing them off. Collect the leftover dust. Double nickels. The financial equivalent of pissing pennies. Wasn't I already high? 4 days, I should probably be biding my time better. Squirreling away for the nighttimes when the lights are brighter and dancing is inevitable. But the whoosh of blah hits my brain and I separate body from it:

Camera raised over head. Ariel. **Arial**. Higher. Out of the blue. Disassociative.

Roland pats his pockets as he steps out of the stall and into the sunshine. A girl with green and purple braids rushes past.

"Ugh, there's no toilet paper," she shouts as the door swings shut behind her. Roland looks back, considering this as somehow his fault for not noticing and notifying the next patron of the bathroom situation. She pushes back out and against him, finding a new spot in line, waiting for one that better suits her needs. The girl scowls at Roland, but he's already forgotten about her. Drugs are known to do that.

Legs outstretched, like that photo of John Lennon (the one with him and Yoko in Cannes, an irredeemable asshole mocking the bow-legged gait of a cowboy fresh off a double wide horse, yee haw pardner heard they got gold down there at Abbey Road).

69

The person that is the self but also outside of and above it, warbles through the droves of people. Not pushing per say but sliding through the hole they create like he's part of a whole 'nother dimension. Where 3 becomes 4. D. Arm extended, out and through passengers on spaceship dirt, Roland stretches himself as thin as possible. Mr. Fantastic. He considers himself a weave. Not only because of the ability to slip through knots and keep himself together, but also because he's able to go by unnoticed, blending in with the flow of the crowd like the rug under the feet of a Persian King.

Limbs fall into the groove before bass fully hits his ears, rounding the bend to the stage, subwoofers still turned the opposite direction toward the woods and 4,000 adoring fans. He can't hear the sound as the Speaker Lords intended, yet he's still drawn to it, straight into the womb of undulating energy. Roland wipes the drip from his nose as he passes deep into the center and merges his body with the collective.

Oh haha. Collective. He gets it now, laughing to himself somewhere between ecstatic and sarcastic. But others join in and it's a hee hee hee hee hee haw haw haw kind of situation. Until there is a camera shoved in his fucking face. Which pulls self back into self even for the briefest moment. Stuck back in skin long enough to not be able to get back out. Gotcha. The Tibetan Book of the Dead ain't got shit on a dude with a camera.

Back in myself. This guy, bearded, hasn't seen a shower in weeks, not to mention days, leans back, lifting one of the three or four cameras hanging around his neck and points it directly at me. I try to shoo him away by throwing up a shoulder but he keeps rotating with me, leaning back on one leg, viewfinder up to his left-right eye, trying to find the perfect shot of me high off me way too high to be photographed for some reason.

"Ah, that's a pretty one. Move it right there. Towards me," he says. I ain't no model on the beach, trying desperately to make the magazine cover. If there was never another photo captured of me ever again I'd be okay with that. Who needs the self-reflexive image stroking? But I pose anyway, mid-laugh, like I'm supposed to, mostly in order to gnat this fly away, but partially because we're literally trained to.

He snaps a couple of photos, switching between cameras until he's satisfied. His body language shifts and he pivots toward me, grabbing and furiously shaking my hand.

"Thank you, thank you, man. Who are you? Who are you?" He laughs, hennheehhheheheh, but doesn't let me answer. "I'm a photojournalist. I've covered the war since '94. I've been at Laos is Beautiful, Coachella, The Burn."

I've stopped dancing. He has a hold on me, gripping my arm into some kind of forceful engagement. "The war?" I ask, fearing the worst by asking any question at all, but also not feeling like I have much else in the way of options.

"The War between Love and Hate, man. The War between Love and Hate. Don't you see all this love, man?" He releases me and gestures around with big wide-open arms. I do. I do see. The faces of people engrossed in a moment fully loving with all of their might.

This is just some spunion with a camera, having an important moment. I can play along. I can let this moment be and not marred by some sourpuss rocked out of his k-hole.

"Fuck Yeah," I say, not adding much, but giving him the validation he needs.

"Fuck Yeah," he responds, echoing me. "Give me a hug brother."

He shoves his body into mine and squeezes as tightly as he can, with complete disregard for the camera-taking technology sandwiched between us. "You get it. You get it." He pauses, like some big revelation is coming. "I mean you wouldn't be *here* [his emphasis] if you didn't, right?" He slaps me on the shoulder, hilarious.

The cameraman gives a thumbs up and makes me assure him that no matter what I won't miss Trevor's set on Monday (like I don't already know that), before disappearing into the crowd to snap more pictures of other beautiful people. "Heady stuff," he leaves me with. As fast as he came into my life he is gone. A flash. But one that put me in a surprisingly good mood.

I check the schedule to see that between Love Language, Dr. Mongoose, and Trevor, I've pretty much gone and signed up for an all-nighter as Sunday turns to Monday, which means that, I guess, Micah is driving home. Tonight, I should— scanning the set times—go to bed after whatever the Beatles is to save face for the final stretch. Why is this so important? I don't know. Something deeply compelling draws me like I couldn't say no if I wanted to.

"Hi," she says, jumping in front of my face with a quick wave and a chipper demeanor. She, her, Noname, woman of my dreams, Manic Pixie Dream Girl (Nathan Rabin, 2005). Is she even really here, or is she just a mirage? Does she even exist at all? Do any of us? Lol.

"Where the heck did you disappear off to last night? I thought we were supposed to daaaaaaaance." She drags the word out for what could last forever if I wanted it to. I imagine it doing exactly that. And it does.

The aaaaaaaaaaaaaaaaaaaaaaaaaaaaaaaaaaaaaaaaaaaaaaaaaaa goes until 2047 when the entirety of Southern California is covered under water. The world hasn't been destroyed yet, but it's well on its way. Aliens have invaded twice and Canada is now Mexico.

The End.

5

"Ronald," I say through gritted teeth.
"Ronald," she repeats in a nearly identical reflection, but with "?" at the end.

"Just some—guy."
"Ah yes I see, the kind of guy you don't want your other friends to meet," she touches her nose as if to say natch. How the fuck do I even know what natch means? Wait, what does it mean? I'm sure I used it correctly. "Well, no time like the present."

She grabs my wrist, pulling me deeper into the dance pit hub's central landing zone. It's not nearly as compact as it looks from the outside, I realize, as we burst through people into our own private bubble. The song changes from something light into something with this massive, pulsating energy, speeding up 3,4,5, Beats Per Minute. I feel each notch moving. Higher and Higher and Higher. Click.

We shake our limbs. Shake them good. Head down, nodding along to the rhythm of the bass. Fingers fluttering to the hi-hats. Synth lines twisting our bodies in and upon each other. We've merged into one. Syncopated union. Church and State no longer separate. Religion is now taught in schools. But, like, everybody's down for it, y'hear?

74

This is nice. I always overthink things so I refuse to think past this being nice. I hold that thought in my brain like an altar. Worship it, repeating it over and over again like it's the only thing that matters in the world. This is nice. This is nice. This is nice. That's all it is. Nothing else to see here, I tell my brain as soon as it wanders away from this path and considers the curve of her hips or the allure in her eyes. This is nice. This is nice.

She intertwines her fingers with mine and my heart skyrockets up and out of my throat, hitting that top bell on the carnival game. Pick a prize, any prize. I'll take the Rastafarian Banana. Oh for me? She asks coyly. I love him. I'll name him Trent and keep on my bedside until we eventually get our own place together and I've no need for an oversized phallic symbol anymore, because I'll have one for my own personal use.

We share eye contact. Eyes had latched together before, but this was our first instance of shared intentional soul-releasing gaze. 4 eyes present and accounted for, two souls behind those eyes communicating without words. This is nice. This is nice.

Noname pulls us closer together, planting her lips on mine. Kissing. This is nice. Kissing is nice. Her tongue runs across the back of my teeth and a rush surges through my body that's somewhere between a rollercoaster and like a really fucking good smoothie.

Vibrations. Energy surrounds us, consuming tongues swirling, people giving us approving thumbs ups without actually doing so. We pull away, drops of spittle stretching between as we separate, trying not to jump each other's bones right here on the dance floor. Which wouldn't be so bad. Approving glances and mental thumbs ups aside, I'm sure we'd put on a hell of a

75

show.

Hey. *Hey.*

We say telepathically. The bubble closes in around us. Feet stepping on foots. Shoulders bumping. Blood surging. Space filling in where we didn't even know we had hoped it wouldn't. I reach through the closing space and pull her toward me. She blinks her eyes in that coy way that might be saying take me now if I was any good at reading that kind of signal. And we run.

Top speed, dodging in and out of dancers, out into the open field behind where the sound is just as nice but we're not trapped by opposing forces closing in on each other until the sound barrier POPS because nothing remains. The sweet spot comfort of the back that many forget, existing because the music is so hypnotic that it draws us all closer. But we've broken that spell.

We find ourselves landing in the grass, bristles of the dry desert attaching themselves to our clothes, but we don't care. Laughing, hands touching in ways that are certainly the precursor to further intimacy. I don't want to talk or kiss, but just stare at this beauty in front of me, exuding an aura that one only reads about in books by men and women that have gone a little too far down the metaphysical rabbit hole. Crustacean Opal. Amethystistic. Purple pressure points signaling out, like the ripples of a fingerprint surrounding her entire two-dimensional presence.

"Who are you?" I ask. She laughs.
"Shut up," stopping my absurd and overly grandiose question.

I don't let this get the best of me, her hand still resting on my thigh, closer to touching my dick than not. "Do you want to go for a walk or something?"

"And miss all the music?" she pulls away, leaning back and closing her eyes. Her head sways to the beat, and whatever seemed like was going to happen is temporarily over. Again, relinquished to momentary celibacy. "I love this song," she adds to a song that doesn't sound particularly unique, before leaping to her feet. "Come on. Come back in there with me." The look of confusion and disappointment on my face must speak massive data sets.

Noname squats down and gets right in my eyeline. There's a sternness in her glare that says look I don't know you and you don't know me we're not gonna fuck in your tent right now no matter how cute I think you are. "Just dance with me you loser."

I snap out of my irredeemable behavior. Appreciate the kindness in this woman, that she recognizes the dumb animal inside me not as scumbaggery but as physical instinct.

Hopping back to my feet, we re-enter the ruckus, doing our best to find that old bubble, or even a new one. But things are different. The music plays loudly as soundtrack to every little thing, but if the beat never changes, how am I supposed to? I shift in my skin.

Mix out: the DJ loops 4/8/16/32 bars of something simple, while bringing in the drums of something else. As they make the loop smaller and smaller it creates this speeding build that needs a cathartic release. At the right moment they drop the first song out and let the second one play through.

The track mixing in is clearly familiar because Noname screams at the top of her lungs. Ahhhh! She grabs my shoulders and hops up and down. "I fucking love you RBCCA" she howls into the void of noise dampened largely by an incredibly powerful speaker system. As if she were a teenybopper grabbing the rail, the boy band du jour stopping in her city. When the first track drops out we're left with a blindingly fast female rapper dropping bars about pussy power.

Power to the pussy, people. It's pussy power. Noname knows every word, dropping low and leaning back on the strangers around us to fully immerse herself in this private performance.

Apropos, I think to myself, slinking slightly back into the faceless crowd. It would be so easy to take two more steps and be gone from this moment. What serves in some unfortunate way as a reminder that I'm not as good of a guy as I always thought I was. Though the reaffirming look she keeps shooting my way tells me that I'm in the clear. Beside the point. Wish there was just something to get me out of my head. And then it hits me…

The spoon, packed full of K hitting my bloodstream, that is. Hunched over in my own bit of space, shoveling another like a gravedigger on his last shift before the all-expenses-paid Hawaiian vacation he won on the radio. KCRX with Jeremy and the Snooze. Coming to you live and direct from The Palace on the Moon. This isn't your average giveaway, no no, this one's for gravediggers only. So gravediggers pick up that phone and give us a call and you'll be flying first class to the Big Island before being whisked away to the luxurious l'Hotel de Mer on the island of Molokini. Shovel faster. Bigger scoops. Bury the dead. Bury yourself.

Yup. Both nostrils snort back simultaneous without a care for what those around me think about my brazen behavior. Lose total track of my love life. In an instant, a full understanding of the word overload, vision twists and fades, knees buckle and the whole world closes in on me. Where is she? I need to sit down. The ground below looks inviting, but the feet dancing around it do not. So I walk backwards, tiny steps that could be the Moonwalk if the brain were connected enough to the body to even know.

Legs betray me. Past the threshold of treacherous stomping feet, and unable to walk any further, I sit. I can feel the whole world rumbling my stomach. Hey! Hey! Fuck you dude! We're trapped in here with too much coffee and no food and we're pissed the fuck off! But. Maybe I'll just take a little nap. Let my head lag a little and sleep this off.

Fuck, I did this to myself. What an idiot. Self sabotager. Cock/block. Always check the spoon. Especially on the double dip. I'd bet big on 8 and 34 that she doesn't even notice anything beyond half a moment that I'm gone before gladly giving up and washing her hands of me.

All I can see behind my eyes is an infinity. A world of mirrors that keep going and has no ending, shifting, moving, rotating. A black, shining ocean of waves. The ground underneath me pitching on angles that no human could stay standing on. Moby Dick attacks. The great white powder. Too much can drive a man mad.

Here I am, furiously laughing at the notion of having to sit out on my own fantasies. I wonder if any actual, legitimate laughter is coming from my body or just in my head. Is my mouth moving or my head lolling on tilt in hysteria. Likely it's just in my lap, dead still, with a pile of puke covering the only pair of jeans I brought with me.

Okay, imagine you are in a hole or a ditch or a tunnel or trapped in a well. Surrounded on most sides by the equivalent of nothing (dirt dark depth etc). There's a light, a beacon, but completely and totally out of reach. There's no climbing out, but instead you must relinquish to the situation of what it is and stay sitting in it because the controlling faculties are trapped in the light too. So what else is there, but to wait it out. Tick tock c'mon clock.

Meditation. Breathe in breathe out om shin ry ki om shin ry ki om—this is all I have left.

Close my figurative eyes. Embrace the dark. Count back from ten to one and repeat any mantra that can get me out of my fucking head. Push out other thoughts. Center. Center. Cent—WHOOSH.

I shoot off into the upper echelons of the astral plane like it ain't no big thing. Casual Nirvana. Doors of Perception. Welcome home friend, stars shooting around me, transforming from stardust right back into entire universes. A mobius strip of everything.

Hello friend. A voice says. An awful lot like Siri, but that's probably only because we push our familiarities onto our hallucinations. I don't have an iPhone, but I still know her vaguely British voice when I hear it.

Welcome to the shared hallucination. The k-hole. The khult. We can all share in this trip together if you help spread the word of peace and love. Overlays of geometric shapes spinning slowly. Opacity

80

all the way up. Faint lines crossing over each other. I stand in the middle, naked and spread. DaVinci's Vitruvian in the crosshair between shapes. *Consume me, Roland. Consume me. It is our great hope to enter your mind and show you all there is to s e e.*

A grand gesture through time and space. Amorphous faceless forms guiding light in times of dark. A titling rubix cube, where each box is a different screen, images flashing, static visuals, turning until they all land on the same thing: a drone shot of Festivalia. Sweeping, robotic shots of the dance floor, bodies still, arms raised up to the heavens. *Praise me.*

K isn't supposed to hit like this. Not like some deep DMT trip, sliding down colorful shapes into the minds of the collective consciousness. Deepening our connection to Earth because of the naturally growing plant this has been extracted from. K is made in a lab. *Ignore the distraction. Open yourself to the 12th realm of the 3rd sector. 62nd Projection, 5th wave.*

I can feel the dirt beneath my legs, shapes of reality forming out of the nothing. Or the nonsense. Or the something in between. Grounded. Quite literally. Hands reach back behind me and lie on the earth. As palms press, I feel the energy of myself surging back upon itself.

Shake it off. Hair hitting the sides of my face and snapping cheeks and eyes and nose back into this present dimension. Whoops. Well that was something. I slowly rise to my feet: a bit more wobbly than usual. Shaky legs. Questionable decisions.

As if my ears wake back up to the music, the techno drops in darker and heavier than anything we'd heard in the last 24. A heavy brass BRAHMMMM that unsettles the already unsettled. A snap decision has me on my feet and pushing through people, bumping hundreds of elbows and nearly knocking over a couple smiling big for a photo.

Glorious, a trash can appears through a gap in the crowd. I weave, sliding behind a guy dressed straight out of *Tron*, a bouncing Ms. Pac Man totem following after. I grip on to the edge of the garbage's plastic frame.

The anxiety of my stomach rears its ugly head, burning the back of my throat—out, instead of in—as bile drips from my mouth, splattering onto the waste below. Those around usher themselves away from my embarrassingly despicable display. Glad Noname isn't here to see this. Would be much much worse than wilting away in front of her. What a putz.

The liquid of my regurgitated coffee rests on top of half-eaten food and empty beer cans. I say hello. We share a moment before I lift myself up with a firm plan of stumbling back to camp.

Electrical currents leaping out of people. Fingertips on fire. This whole place could go up in a flash of flame if we aren't careful with all this static excitement our bodies are conducting, passing by and rubbing, creating currents that flicker in the air. A palpable energy verbalized by all those around me in mutters and shrieks of excitement. Passerby weave to the sides, as I trudge along, falling with every heavy step, just trying to make it home.

Make way for me please thank you very much. And those on their way down, while I, on my way up, do exactly what is hoped of them. A kind service I thank with a half-pulled together smile stretched and strained but that's okay because it's the thought that counts.

Pass Do and say Hello. Consider stopping for a while with Lyle. A can of beer and a bit of a sit should set me right by rain that's what, for sure, for certain. No rush to the next thing.

Before I even make sight of our camp I hear Micah exclaiming: "man, you look terrible." Turn the head ever so slightly to see my friend in the exact same spot I left him so many hours ago. Days?

"Yeah," is all I can mutter, plopping next to him and fishing in our cooler for a can of carbonated alcohol water. The cold water (and the remnants of ice) send a wakeup call through my body. Military bugle boy signaling it's time for drills, but I'm cracking open one of thirty overpriced low-quality beers. PBR. Miller Lite. Bud Light. Coors. Tecate. They're all the same and anyone who says otherwise must be an expert in nuance.

I sip and my stomach fills where there was once an absence. Is this the best solution for having just relieved said chamber of all it had previously contained? Don't know. Don't care. Sometimes it's all about forward momentum and following instincts instead of what's right. Food was probably the answer, but I wasn't about to order a Bacon fried Cheeseburger with strands of vomit hanging off my lip. Gotta get better before I can get out.

"You make it in?" I ask.
Micah laughs. Huunnh. Likely because he knows how funny I'll think it is that he hasn't.
"Made about as far as that six-foot bong halfway down the hill."

"Lyle."
"Yup. They kept packing him. I kept smoking. Got too stoned to function. Had to crawl my way back here for some trail mix." Without barely moving Micah grabs the plastic bag of nuts and assorted accoutrements off the ground and offers it to me.

I lean over and take the bag from him, popping open this zipper much more easily than I'm able to with drug bags 1/128th its size. Plus with the pink lines, this one's industrial strength. Probably paid extra at Trader Joes or Whole Foods just for the security that a bear couldn't get into it if he tried. Now that's real camping.

A handful of nuts and raisins and these awesome little peanut butter sticks travel from the bag to my mouth via the contraption where I temporarily convert my hand into a scoop. I crunch away, transforming the proteins into smaller, digestible versions that will surely turn this upset tummy situation around.

"Put myself into a k-hole and puked."

Hunnnhunh. Micah laughs again, too stoned for anything outside of one or two drawn out throat vibrations. An intonation that I know all too well. I continue, knowing I have a rapt audience and spin yarns about blowing it with Noname twice in the span of 24 hours. Some kind of expert at girls thinking I'm a full-on fool.

We conclude—as they say in textbooks—that third time's a charm. Redelivering the phrase ad nauseum in the voice of as many wrestlers from our past as we can conjure up. Third times a charm, Brother! Can you smell what the third time's a charm is cookin'? Cause Stone Cold says third time's a charm. It's a meaningless term, which carries no actual weight, but we give it weight anyways. If only to make me feel better in this moment of weakness. This self-reflexive infinity chamber of positive affirmation is why we keep friends around anyways. Woo.

I want to formulate a plan that has me and Micah spreading out and combing the dance floor inch by inch until Noname turns up, but it feels foolhardy and vain. And psychopathic. Plus, this body is in no condition to exert beyond scooping another handful of mixtrail into face.

"What time is it?" I ask, like it matters. Micah doesn't check a phone or a watch for an answer, but rather looks up to the sky like a true nomad living off the land. Sunshine lad, the human dial. The sun has broken behind trees, settling in for the beginnings of its slumber if not quite there yet. Adjacent to the brink of its set. He extends his arm, squints with one eye and comes up with a definitive answer: "7:15." He follows up with a "Yeah, 7:15, 7:20" confirming his confidence. "7:30."

"What time is Paul McCartney on?" I ask, sounding pathetic, not only in delivery, but in subject matter. What am I, just here for the headliner? Come on.

Micah must have taken some base memorization class that wasn't offered in my formative years, because he's able to whip out the answer frighteningly fast. As if it were already waiting at the tip of his tongue. Like he knew what question I was going to ask and was rearing to say the word 'ten' regardless of what emerged from my mouth. Or he was just excited too. I mean why shouldn't we be excited.

This, on some level, was why we are all here. Because the Beauty Collective boys shine enough on their own to get us to trust them and buy tickets to their festivals. Their sets stand heads above the crowd, seven and a half feet tall, towering giants of talent. Make the music matter where it might not've much.

I guess it's not about the music 'til it is, 5,000 dancing to the second coming of one of pop-music's major icons. Sure, he's not as good of a songwriter as the actual McCartney, but he still has this pop-sensibility that's unmatched (and frankly unheard of) in house music. Writing hits that never feel cheesy, but you could play for your Mom and she'd go oh that's nice.

Okay, I admit it. I'm a person too. I wanted to be there. Sort of almost nearly had to be. The rest of the weekend wouldn't sit right if I didn't hit that first act break properly. So with two and a half hours in front of me, I had to make a plan. Sitting here with Micah was not an option or I'd just keep railing K and the hours would pass and I'd wake up in this chair with the rise instead of the set thinking what the fuck happened and where did I go wrong, realizing it was this moment right here that was necessary in turning the tides.

The plan consists of the following things (in order?):

- ☐ Chill for a bit longer, nursing this beer and maybe another one—but not a third;
- ☐ Get some food: preferably something on the fresher/healthier spectrum with enough protein quality to keep me going for at least a couple of hours. Can't subsist on only beer and cocaine and liquor and psychedelics like I used to, leaving weekends in the desert ten pounds lighter from eating like a goddamn bird;
- ☐ Change my clothes and wash my body (likely in reverse order). The combination of sun and puke and dirt has my skin crawling and this brief moment of respite is a surefire guarantee of an opportunity to change my outlook for the entirety of the night;
- ☐ Brush my teeth too;
- ☐ Do some combination of the drugs in my pocket. Maybe even try and rustle up a dose and see where that takes me—though if I want to sleep tonight (and not tomorrow) maybe L isn't the best idea, reframe; do some combination of the drugs in my pocket;
- ☐ Head to the dance floor—with or without Mica. It

seems unlikely that he'll join me on the stretch that is this mission, but also with this slow-ass sloth maybe our timelines will line-up just right and by the time I'm brushing my teeth and blowing some coke Micah's waking up from the nap that is his life ready and raring to go to see Paul McCartney II;

□ Out amongst the music I will ditch my friend and pursue Noname until... man, I dunno.

And then I do all those things.

When it's all said and done and I'm prepped and ready to hit execute on the final task Micah is nowhere to be found. Which sucks because I need his frog spoon in order to do drugs. Except, what have I been doing them with? Shit, I'm not exactly sure. As last mentioned—now that I'm slightly more clear-headed and tracking things—the key to my car was left securely in my tent (still safe and sound I'm sure, but even taking the chance to check would only offer me the opportunity to lose it, so I don't and just trust in the universe), and though I had been using Micah's spoon I don't actually have one of my own. I realize that I don't have a spoon and on a subsequent rewrite I must go back and write one into existence for myself (please turn back to page 59 (the appropriate opportunity) to see if that happened or not).

Or maybe I just do it here.

One magically appears in the cupholder of my collapsible chair. It's 24K gold and covered in rhinestones along the petite handle. 4 bumps. Two of each. Two in each bag. One in each nostril. Like a crisscross-applesauce pattycake switcheroo and I'm ready to go back to the dance floor, self-assured in a way that can only be supplanted by a drug that makes one feel a bit like a superhuman and another one that makes one feel like nothing at all.

Sorry for the speed talking, it was the speed talking.

The next part is where things veer off. Cause it's dark and everything changes as the light goes away, slowly behind mountains sure, but away still. The night is where all our preconceived notions of what is and isn't going to happen are thrown out the window, careening down the highway never to be seen again.

New lights have replaced daylight. Neon headbands and earrings, dresses and scarves, bits of wire run across hats and sleeves and socks and bicycle tires. Signs, hand made, but intricately designed. Who Cares? Pictures and phrases and designs intended as beacons of familiarity. The singularity of this blue neon spiral on top of a pole will lead all that know it to the same spot on the dance floor. No crew? No need for light.

I step onto the main drag and the Ren Faire vibe has shifted as many generations into the future as the Renaissance was in the past. Science Fictional. Where people need effervescent light to see through the night because all building infrastructure has been ravaged and we must live off the lay of the land. Savages and scavengers resort to unspeakable deeds to protect the people they are camped with. People pass me by, buzzing with the anticipation of all the rumors they've heard about Festivila's wild debauchery coming to be true.

Saturday people tripping, dropping acid, and falling all over themselves, asking me the way to the stage. I point and they take the opposite direction. A complete and utter disregard for how things are supposed to be. But I guess that's their prerogative, zonked out in lysergic bliss, too young to care about the implications of not knowing where their campsite is come the desperate search later. They'll either end up dancing not a care in the world until the sun comes up and the way back is as clear as day, or they'll crawl into some tent or corner thanks to the overwhelming kindness of strangers.

So I follow my own direction, or the one of sound getting louder, in the physical representation of the < symbol. I look out onto the swarming, packed, dance floor with a thousand individual blinking, flashing, moving lights and I'm instantly lost, pulled into an unreality that can only be made real again by the passage of time.

Eyes adjust, but only to immediate surroundings. To my left a small woman paints a tiger swallowing the soul of the man, and the man swallowing the soul of the tiger in return. It's a yin yang, but also the circle of life, and maybe even a statement about the impermanence of existence, reincarnation, and how if you strip it all back, we're all essentially one.

In front a couple with goggles (unnecessary) and decked in leather from head to toe (kinky) grinds on each other. I don't know if they're about to fuck or they just did, but with his tongue down her throat as far as it is, they're certainly entertaining.

Behind me a group of dudes hold a bag of wine over each other's heads. They take turns slapping it, each one more vicious than the last, before dropping down below the spigot and releasing the biggest gulp or seven into their mouths. The dudes say nothing in particular, but egg each other on with grunts and pats and sniffs and snorts.

To my immediate right: another dude, alone, bobbing his head to the beat, reminding me of my presence here, a man by himself who looks just like any other man by himself. Is he having a good time? Am I? Why isn't he dancing harder? Am I dancing at all? Look down to my feet, hips shaking, toes tapping along with the beat: the bare minimum to be considered 'getting down.' This mirror reflection of myself is both endearing and off putting. I can't shake it.

Take a few steps forward for a change of scenery and an instantaneous change of energy. More people compact, dancing to what I can only assume is T.U.R.B.o., but I refuse to take my phone out and confirm set times and or time times.

EDM is a dirty word. One maligned by just about every person who has been involved in the scene longer than a year. Electronic Dance Music has become the catch-all for the type of Big Room Pop that has made it to the radio: Zedd, The Danger Brothers, Central Horse Mafia.

The catch then becomes having a subgenre that you call home. The list goes on and on from house to trance to techno to dubstep to drum & bass to downtempo. But then it gets even narrower. Booty House and Psytrance, Minimal Techno and Midtempo, Jump Up and Trip Hop. Breaks, Acid, Garage, Jungle, Hardstyle, Glitch, Wobble, Detroit, Chicago, Goa, Jersey, Trap, Tribal, Disco—the list goes on with just about any combination of the aforementioned you could possibly imagine.

Some of these genres are more technically engaging than others. Big Room radio EDM has the drop. The DROP: the moment where the song changes into some big swelling bombastic electro energy. There's usually singing over the hook but the drop is just the drop. Can't miss the drop in dubstep with bass slamming in so forcefully the whole world is forced to pay attention. Commanding ears through metal crunching inspired sound-design. Metal-metal and \m/ metal.

This is what molly-munchers chase. That is until their serotonin reserves are tapped permanently and they need to find another way to enjoy this kind of music (or abandon it completely, which happens to many, gladly returning to guitars and radio hip-hop).

But for the rest of us, there's always something else, and that something varies from person to person. Some get into DJing—or just buying modular synths and never actually doing anything with them—but the rest of us find a place or genre or scene or message board that requires more patience and can be enjoyed on less substances. I fuck with house. Beauty Collective plays both house and techno. I don't mind techno, but I'm partial to house.

House is about finding the groove and sticking with it. The drums are always more-or-less the same, kick, hi-hat, kick. Over and over again, changing up only when the artist feels like throwing in a breakbeat or taking a quick interlude over to something else entirely. Silence for one.

The groove, the funk, the bass, is constantly changing. But a good DJ keeps that groove going smoothly between tracks. So while it's changing, you're changing with it. Caught on a life raft out at sea, sure it moves with the waves, but you've become one with it. You move too.

What else is there to do when you can't find the girl of your dreams, but catch that groove and ride it? T.U.R.B.o., though his name wouldn't necessarily inspire it, is a very groove-oriented DJ. Smooth sailing. Keep it chill and ride the waves. My instinct upon first hearing his name (without hearing any of his music) was that he'd sound more robotic, engines raring, speed, techno, but that just goes to show that you can't judge anything by its title—*Good at Drugs?*, yeah right.

§

Paul McCartney is pretty good. He's always perfectly reasonably pretty acceptably good. Does he live up to my expectations? Sure. What are those tricky things even? I wish I could give more, but I really can't do better than that. There's a reason why I never amounted to much as a music blogger. Rave reviewer. Whatever.

He performs much as I've seen him perform before, singing love ballads—into the mic—as if he's stuck writing cut-rate songs for a third-string version of Wings. Except without the backing band. Sure, this sometimes results in him missing a transition or two, but the kindly looking man in the suit with the greying temples is so ingratiating that nobody really minds.

He really does look like the actual Paul. Eerily so. Though there's something about his sound that doesn't quite compute. Like these things should work together on paper, but every time they kind of don't. Translating spanish to english then back to spanish. Paul McCartney II is likely the worst of the four but endearing in his own way. Fun is had and then it is over.

His set goes dark, cut out and settling into the kind of epic silence that would only come before fucking Black Sabbath are set to take the stage or something. Everybody around me is jazzed. A palpable hush that's so thick people are likely to flip their lids. Nobody knows what's going to happen next. And that's very very intoxicating. I don't even need more drugs. Okay, maybe a little coke.

Fog pours out of the smoke machine. Or is it smoke from the fog? Out amongst us, the people, filling the ether, the space between until we're all covered in a thin haze. A voice comes through the speakers, lo-fi with the white noise rattle of a very old recording turned up louder than it has any right to be. Is that Ed Sullivan?

"England. September of 1963 we first heard the Beatles and signed them right there on the spot. Ringo Starr, Paul McCartney, John Lennon and George Harrison."

Flash of white strobe lights hitting the stage in one smoothly executed movement is followed by a single scream from somewhere in the audience. More of a hoot really, breaking the tension, causing some to laugh and others to tense up in even more excitement. I peer over heads looking for the source, but just see a sea of hats and hair. A long drawn out pause before Ed Sullivan continues: "Ladies and Gentlemen, The Beatles."

Lights up. Everybody screams, hands to cheeks, doing their best impression of the teenage girls on the loose in 1964 New York City. This makes me think of Noname. I don't even know why really, but when I see Love Language, TimeCop, Trevor and Paul McCartney step out on stage in full Sgt. Pepper's regalia I can't help but throw thoughts away and let myself be taken over by the moment.

"Woo! Yeah!," I scream at the top of my lungs, even adding a

"Hell Yeah!" for good measure.

The foursome step to the decks waving—royal, cupped hands—before dropping in on a remix of Lucy in the Sky with Diamonds. Jealous of those high on LSD as they picture themselves on a boat on a river, with tangerine trees and marmalade skies. The couple next to me have their eyes closed in what I can only imagine is a head full of gorgeous hallucinations based on the dumbstruck smiles on their faces.

There are some things that are once in a lifetime experiences; that can't be captured again. This could happen year after year until the end of this festival's run, but it wouldn't, couldn't, pack the same punch as this. The unknown—

A set full of Beatles tunes perfectly remixed in tune to the Beauty Collective sound. Blackbird singing in the dead of night take these broken wings and learn to fly fly fly fly untz untz untz. The drum breaks from Come Together laid out into a consistent four on the floor beat, an anthem that could be played at every sporting event from here on eternity. We scream about being able to work it out, getting by with a little help from our friends, and how our troubles felt so far away, yesterday.

Grab a brother or sister next to me—don't even look—swaying in perfect accompaniment to the horn-driven repetition of love love love, building a beat with a fresh slap of Trevor's all too familiar sound design and we all believe for one simple, uncomplicated moment that truly, all you need is love.

All together now.

Awestruck, mouth agape, dazed and confused on a psychedelic

journey through hit after hit from the band that those without any discerning taste cite as their favorite. That's because, I guess, as is revealed to us over the course of these sacred 120 minutes, they really are the best there ever was.

Who gets credit here? The curator or the innovator? The reinventor or the originator? Ain't that the charm of the remix?

Music feels reinvented. Like we can start all over from here. That there will be a Before and After the Beauty Collective play The Beatles. BC. Before Christ. Beauty Collective. Beatles Christ.

Time slips by and the minute hands start to not stretch as slowly anymore. Nervous feet patter as people check cell phones and watches confirming sneaking suspicions that this paradise is not long for. 1:49AM. Ten minutes remain, as they kick into Here Comes the Sun, stripped down to its original elements and just left alone to play as is. It's beautiful, sweeping, and though the sun is long gone, we can feel its warmth encompassing us.

The song fades out and there's a pause. A brief interim of silence. Oh no, is that it? It can't! It mustn't be! The show literally has to go on.

The vocals come back before any instrumentation, rip-roaring out of the speakers like they're being howled through the microphone at the edge of the known universe. When I get to the bottom, I go back to the top of the slide. Where I stop and I turn and I go for a ride til I get to the bottom and I see you again.

White noise fills in the empty space, hammered by drums in

a high-energy brokenbeat patterning, The iconic guitar riff, converted into a fluctuating, shimmering bass groove, leads way to a break where the repetition of Helter Skelter has the whole dance floor headbanging. Helter Skelter. Helter Skelter. Helter Skelter. Woo.

Boom, back into the drums and we're all jumping and bouncing, laughing, and landing. We're all on top of each other and not minding in the goddamn least. The Beauty Collective suceed in capturing the speed and manic energy of this one, converting it into the craziest drum & bass weapon this side of 1994.

When they finish and the song cuts out as suddenly as it came in, we all collapse to the ground. 5,000 people in the world's most geeked up cuddle puddle, rolling around in the dirt like one 20,000 limbed animal loving every second of it.

Love Language lifts the microphone, and in his best attempt at a British accent says, "Thank You America, Good Night!" Boom! The Helter Skelter (Drum & Bass Remix) ramps back up for one last drop. We leap to our feet and shake it out for the track's final spin.

The boys leave the stage, and we stand, shook, unable to compose ourselves. Faces completely melted off of skeleton and muscle and skin. Piles of the artist formerly known as face oozing below our feet. The energy so goddamn unified, a force for good in the world so unique and streamlined that there was no feeling amongst this mass of us other than astonished awe and amazement.

A voice through the mic: "Uh, I don't really know how to follow that." We laugh. "So I guess I'm just gonna play some...

normal tunes." A simple tech-house beat comes out of the speakers, and people start dispersing like the whole event is over, gaps in the crowd eating swiss cheese. I feel bad for the dude on stage, but also don't because I feel good about myself having experienced a moment so transcendent and full of joy. I'm sure deep down he does too.

Those of us who remain are shocked into submission. Ramped up and raring to go, but no idea what to do with ourselves. A dude in an oversized bomber jacket and harem pants paces in a circle. "What the fuck! What the actual FUCK!?" he shouts up to the heavens with ecstatic rage. He stops in front of me, and playfully shoves me with palms outstretched.

"What the hell was that!?" he asks.
"Uhhhhhhhhhhhhhh," I respond, not having an answer, but letting the drawn-out nature of not having an answer be my answer.

"Exactly Exactly! Anybody sleeping through that just made the world's biggest mistake! You're an idiot, Squirrel!" He mimes answering a phone. "Uhhhh, hello, yeah it's Lexi. What did you miss? Oh man, only the best goddamn motherfucking piece of shit set in the entire known UNIVERSE. Yeah, yeah, hold on. This guy wants to talk to you." He hands the nonexistent phone to me.

I play. I can play. I know how to play. It might take a couple rotations around my brain for me to realize it, but I am capable of play. I play.

Hello? I say into the phone, starting in on a bit where the guy on the other end of the phone is being a tough guy, but I can be a tough guy too. Oh tough guy, you think you're so tough?

I'm here with my friend and we're telling you you're done for. You've lost. Cooked. You missed the magic. And there's nothing no two-bit jerk like you can do about it. I hang up the phone furiously and throw it in the dust. "He was really rude."

My new friend in the harem pants picks up his nonexistant phone and mimes brushing it off. "Sorry, that guy can be a real dickhead sometimes." He extends a hand. I grab it. We exchange names as our hands pass through air on a vertical spectrum. *Lexi.* Roland. *Like the sequencer?* Yeah. How was that for you? Life-changing. Exactly. Stole the words right out of my mouth.

Lexi pulls his hand away repeating "hold up, hold up, hold up," dropping the backpack off his shoulder and letting it collide with the ground. He unzips and reaches inside to pull out a bag of red wine. Half full. I can tell from this half-filled alcoholic juice pouch that this is the Franzia brand cabernet sauvignon. "Vino?" he asks excitedly, bestowing the best gift in his arsenal for a new dance-floor acquaintance.

I can't let Lexi down. He bounces with energy, good vibe incarnate, the happy one—ain't nothing gonna break-a his stride, ain't nothing gonna hold him down, oh no. So I say yes thank you, by pulling my arm back and slamming the hell out of the plastic bag. It spins in place, whipping around itself to catch its breath again. When it stops back in my general vicinity, I pull it close and unleash the beast.

He hands the bag to me expecting a quid pro quo of holding it up for him. I do. And he slaps the bag like a newborn baby wake up call to the world. Hello, the plastic SLAP screams and wails. The pour that follows is longer than any pee I've ever taken, even the really long ones. How he can hold that much at one time, I'm not sure, but he keeps guzzling anyways and guzzling and guzzling some more.

Eventually he pulls away, closes the mouthpiece, and takes the bag back. After Lexi zippers it up in his backpack he looks at me like I have the answers. I don't. My mind's still fully blown from that set and I haven't had to account for a rave baby in years. There's definitely a sense of 'what's next' oozing from this young buck. Tell me wise old sage where shall I go after that?

Staying here doesn't feel like an option. We try and listen to the music, catch in, but after a set as transcendent as The Beatles II, everything sounds about as plain as flavorless ice cream. Dripping off the cone, but it mostly tastes like air. And no matter how many licks, you're left unsatisfied consuming the empty calories.

We walk in unison, almost by accident. Leaving the set later than either of us had intended, his friends gone, mine never found, forming a bond in our inability to follow the herd. We head the same direction, toward our similar, but separate destinations, the trail back to camp as empty as the dancefloor. Last ones back after the mad dash of rush-hour traffic. The conversation flows quickly toward the generic as silence looms over our collaborative journey, kicking dust up in the air as our feet take hold on the dusty trail.

Where are you from? I say San Diego and he tells me LA. I tell him that I used to live in LA and he wants to know what part. Echo Park, but he lives in Venice, and we both know those are completely different cities so there's no taking that thread further.

Have you ever been to one of these before? I tell him what it was like 5 years ago with hardly any food, one vendor, barely any, art and about an eighteenth of the lights and production. He's been to a couple of the all-night warehouse parties they threw downtown, but nothing like this.

I thank the Lord Xenu that he doesn't ask what I do. These rave babies always think jobs matter, that they're all something exciting like personal trainers or cryptocurrency advisors. I write the Twitter posts for a brand of food he's certainly heard of. People always think it's cool but it's not. It's all the way not cool. Hate feeling partially to blame for the never-ending data suck. The never content with content scroll. A side hustle that I treat like the real hustle, so it doesn't seem to amount to much more of a paycheck than food and rent and internet and a couple weekends of abandon here and there. Thought by 30 I'd be someone special.

The road hits an impasse and we each can sense the other splitting off into separate directions. I go in for a hug, and a pre-emptive 'alright dude' as if to say well it's been real.

I take two steps away before Lexi asks the magic question.

"Do you know anyone who needs some L?"

5

Yeah, I know a guy. And that guy's name is Roland. Me, that guy. Me need LSD. Who what where when why how much? He answers the questions in reverse order. But to reframe them as a sentence: If I come to his campsite just up the hill, his buddy Squirrel is selling doses for like ten bucks a hit. Yes. Yes! Score!

As we walk into unfamiliar territory, where the tents are different brands and there are far more trees making nightshade from the moonlight, I ask Lexi what kind of high we're talking about. The phrase "acid is acid," is not what I'm looking for. Not all acid is created equal.

There are notes and nuances that separate the exact same goddamn chemical compound. I like to consider these little touches the flair of the person behind the piano, more-so than the composer. Like the drug can feel the fingers it passes through and reflect a trip thusly.

Lexi says all the right things. The key phrases and buzzwords that tell me he too is an aficionado of the finer things. Fluff. Clean. Light visuals. Not too heady. Hint of nutmeg.

"I've got some coke and K," I tell him.
He snorts, excited. "My man. Our kind of people."

103

Aren't we all our kind of people? Just by showing up, I feel like we're all bound to get along to some degree. This feels reasonable although idealistic. But then again, where else do you meet instantaneous friends on the dance floor? There may be no place more justified toward idealism than these pockets of temporary society built by those wanting to shake it loose with those willing to shake it loose alongside them. It all feels simple when we're here. Why's it so hard when we're out there?

Lexi pulls back a tie-dye sheet into a well-lit pocket of warmth. Fives dudes and two chicks sit huddled in a small open space under tarps and tapestries dangling a few inches above their heads. It's a stark juxtaposition to Hampton's purchased palace, mine and Micah's homely, but dialed-in abode, or any number of the trust-funded campsites that come with all the accoutrements to not only survive, but thrive, for days out in the desert.

"Heyyy" they all say one after the other. A round of hellos. Merrily, merrily, life is but a dream.

Lexi introduces me around his squad. Beth, Gene, Paul, Squirrel, Starchild, Detroit, and Cris. They smile and wave and invite me to take a seat in one of the empty chairs. They remind me of crews I've been fortunate enough to hit these things with in the past. Friends forever we said then, but now all we have are some shared memories and a whole lot of things left unsaid. We still call each other best friends, but rarely reach out. Sad sorta.

They're all so young. Gotta be like 22, 24. Bright-eyed ravers, taking that big turn from hotel rooms and spectacle to community. Ecstasy to psychedelics. The inevitable switch from what we seem unable to return.

Loose cigarette butts sit in the open mouths of empty beer cans. I flick one inside and hear it land at the bottom. Detroit continues telling everyone about Movement—the Detroit techno festival that 'changed his life.' Everybody has to go next year. I wonder if he's from Detroit, and that's where he got his nickname, or if it's sort of a patronizing thing because he won't stop talking about it. I decide not to ask.

"You want a beer?" Cris asks, lifting herself off the cooler to fish one out for me. I thank her and take the beer, crack the top and let that cool liquid hit my throat. I try not to drink during the day—daring to say after starting my day off with one—but goddamn if that after-rave beer isn't the most refreshing thing in the entire existence of refreshments.

Cris asks if any others want a beer, but I turn my attention to business. So I hear you got acid, I ask the one dressed like a squirrel.

Squirrel says the same things that Lexi had earlier. Clean, fluff. That's all I ever want. We discuss the downsides of too heady acid and he tells me a story from Electric Racetrack where he was frying face and his crew abandoned him at the Weirdless stage. Went down a series of dark wormholes he couldn't get out of. Why he sources his shit better now.

"You want it now?" he asks, reaching for his side satchel. "Trying to see the sun come up?"
"No, no. Tomorrow. But ya boy seemed legit, and I don't sneeze at a good connect."
"For sure, for sure."
"Though, I do kind of wish I was tripping for that Beatles set."

Lexi's eyes light up. "Hell Yeah!" he adds, but nothing further.

Some of the others grumble. Beth chimes in, a short girl with short hair in the corner. "I thought it was stupid. If I wanted to listen to old-people music I'd hang out with my Dad."

I laugh, feeling my age. "Haha, I guess I'm old as hell then." They all laugh, which tells me more about how out-of-place I must look than anything. Forgetting to grow up, still pretending to be something I barely scratched the surface at a decade ago. It wasn't supposed to be that funny.

"What are you, 30?" Gene or Paul asks, two white dudes with beards and longish shaggy hair. I likely couldn't tell them apart with a gun against my head and someone screaming in my ear to get it right or they'll kill everyone I've ever known.

"'Bout that. 31. How old are y'all?" Various answers come in one by one: 22, 23, 24. Damn Lexi is young. Just turned 21 a week ago. Geez. Squirrel claims to be 28, but I don't really believe him. 26, maybe. The patriarch of the clan. Daddy LSD. But then again, a man dressed in a squirrel suit (not just like a onesie, but a seemingly fully functional tail with impressive craftsmanship on a hat (helmet?) that looks about as realistic as it gets. The squirrel eyes even blink!) definitely has some regressive tendencies to work through. Young for his age.

He tells me his story while filling out my order. 5 hits—not all for me, probably give one or two to Micah if he's down to join me on a journey through time and space.

"One day I was 'tripping balls' in the middle of the park, staring up at the trees." Familiar. Nothing more powerful than being high on psychedelics and witnessing slight movements

106

occurring in nature. Because this isn't a hallucination, we're just open to noticing it now. While under the influence. I know the sensation well. Trying to buy it actually.

He pauses, with mini scissors in hand, cutting a row of perforated tabs off a much larger sheet. "When this squirrel comes out on the branch and stops, looking me directly in the eyes like we're communicating, I knew: I am a squirrel." He blurts it out one more time after a long pause, staring off into space and considering his animal existence. "I am a squirrel."

"Cool," I say as he hands me my doses, folded up in some extra tinfoil to keep them at their tip-top shape for tomorrow.

"$40 bucks," Squirrel says, back in the transaction. I reach into my back pocket and fish out the cash.

"You want a bump of K?" I ask, handing him the money. Squirrel nearly hippity hops out of his seat. Leave it to the man who's become one with the animals to get absolutely amped about an animal tranquilizer.

I take a bump for myself before passing the bag. Squirrel offers to the others, but most decline. He hands it to Starchild who looks to me for approval before hitting the bag. I give him a nod. Starchild lifts up the silver visor from his helmet and takes two petite sniffs, one in each nose, before passing it to Lexi. Lexi elbows me for attention.

"How much should I…?" He trails off, afraid to finish the sentence and admit that he doesn't know what he's doing. I appreciate the kid's candor. Not afraid to ask for help instead of taking too much and becoming a burden on all his friends. In my command, the spoon digs in bite-sized compared to

107

what it'd been doing, pulling out about a third of my usual allotment.

Anybody who doesn't know their own dosage definitely doesn't need that much. Carefully now, egg on a spoon, move the powders up to his nostril. He snorts, thanks me, and leans back in his chair.

Starchild asks if I have any more for sale. We're not all so lucky as to have the right drug dealer in our midst. Never understood why Hampton didn't sell acid though. I tell him that I know a guy and I'll ask next time I see him, but. We make plans how to find this campsite if I do. I have no recollection of how I got here, blindly following Lexi through the trees

Up the path, turn right at the barber pole, stop at the tapestry of Jimi Hendrix's face and come on in. Different from my important landmarks: Do and Lyle, but same basic point. He grabs the back of Jimi's face with his hand as if to point out the print he's talking about. I swear someone could make a killing if they invested in some new tapestry prints. Been using the same designs to block out the sun since before Hendrix put a ten-strip on the inner lining of his bandana and let sweat do the work.

I repeat the directions to myself to try and make them stick. Up the path, Right at the barber pole, Jimi Hendrix. Right at the barber pole, Jimi Hendrix. This is more for show and good faith than anything. Forgetting is half the fun.

With the little rectangle of tinfoil stored securely away in my wallet and these people who have likely known each other for years, separating off into smaller conversations about third parties and inside jokes, I figure it's time to hit the dusty trail.

Beer finishing o'clock. I'm not one to leave a wounded soldier behind, waste someone's hard-earned $1 to $3 depending on how bad of a deal they got. Once the last and final drops drip onto my tongue, I understand that my time here is done.

I bid my new friends adieu. Squirrel, Lexi, Beth, Detroit, Starchild, Cris, Gene and Paul all get separate moments of recognition, thanking Squirrel personally for the hallucinogen and offering each of the others some slight variation on 'hope I see you out on the dancefloor tomorrow.' With Lexi, I think he knows I actually mean it, instead of the customary one the rest get.

He can barely get his words out straight, smiling up at me in ketamine bliss. With that look on his face I can more-or-less guarantee his ass finds me tomorrow looking for more.

I walk home with a pocket full of acid, psyched on my prospects. Should it have been this easy? Yes. Modern drugs ain't so hard to find if you know where to look.

Micah's already asleep when I make my way back into our sectioned off corner of the world. I can hear the electrical buzzsaw of his snore through the thin fabric of his tent. I laugh, thinking about the other tents around us. People trying to sleep and the music coming from the speakers dwarfed by my friend's fucked up nasal passages.

Never wake someone asleep on Xanax. It's just going to end poorly. A fist to the face, a wrestling match on rocky terrain, maybe just angry, bitter glances for a year and a half. Looks like there were no benzos for me tonight. I'd have to find sleep the way cavemen did, by counting wooly mammoths.

109

I take a seat in our little living room. It's built for two, tapestries and tents strategically placed to keep in warmth. The festival common area is one that only gets better with years of practice and accumulation of stuff. That is, if the wind doesn't come and rip it all right out of the ground.

Those kids showed promise. I might actually search them out tomorrow, take them under my wing. Become gramps to Squirrel's Daddy. All I had remaining from my once-and-powerful crew of festival-going friends is Micah. Though 110 of us had camped together at our absolute peak. Maybe some fresh blood was what was needed in my life to get the spark back.

But then again, I had to see about a girl.

And some psychedelics.

Big plans, big plans.

As I dream about a tomorrow that hasn't yet happened, I feel my eyes closing on me. Instincts follow my body to the tent. Once comfortable and ready for lights out, I give myself a huge rip of K and ease into sleep through the hole. Again. Same as it ever was.

SUNDAY

A friend once imparted on me the phrase Psychedelic Sunday.
As if it were a proper noun. One that was a fact, and not a
suggestion, for those of us well-practiced. That psychedelics
were first and foremost a sacrament meant for the holy day.
But also because Friday and Saturday had passed, and you, I,
we, they, us, now knew this map like the back of our hand.

What restraint I'd shown. For two whole days at a RAVE,
MUSIC FESTIVAL, PARTY, TRANSFORMATIONAL
FUNCTION, BE-IN, whatever, I hadn't been tripping my
fucking face off. How deeply unfortunate.

Sure, people had to drive places on Monday, but some of that
acid afterglow was necessary for the legendary 5+ hours that
the Beauty Collective would spin back-to-back to close things
out. A head full of acid should get me all the way through the
Love Language and TimeCop B2B late-night set and to Dr.
Mongoose's sunrise thing. I wasn't going to imagine myself
into this one, I was going to make damn sure of it.

This all comes to me, downloaded, sitting slouched in a
collapsible camping chair (green) while my partner in crime
(Micah) sits in another (blue). I fiddle with the patch of tinfoil,
turning it over in my hands like it will unleash some sort of
hidden knowledge. Hit the right button and the Dybbuk Box

111

will open to reveal all things. Micah rolls a joint.

Pinching weed together into a perfect cone, turning the paper carefully to catch the ground green, Micah leans to it and licks the edge of the wrapper. He folds over and wraps it up in the smooth motion of a figure skater. Between two pinched fingers, the joint looks like the kind you'd buy in a store. And nowadays I guess you sort of would. Three days a week, Micah does exactly this for a dispensary. Supplemental income and a proper discount comes about out to a living wage. But it's also the living equivalent of the old lady hunched over her sewing machine, back bent in discomfort, mending a hemline or a cuff or a t-shirt pocket. It's only not a sweatshop if they pay you right, apparently.

Flame to the tip, and Micah ignites, smoke entering his lungs, doing a lap or two around the old shriveled husks before settling into the sensitive part of flesh and becoming the guiding principle of what makes him normal again.

He shakes his head and puffs, letting the joint slowly disappear in front of his lips. He doesn't bother to offer it to me, which I appreciate. I know I could ask if I wanted.

The joint dwindles down to nothing, a little roach held between pinched fingers. Micah crosses his legs, puts the burning embers out on the heel of his shoe and turns to me. "Okay, I'm ready."

I turn the tinfoil in my hand and unwrap it as quickly as I can. Fingers catching under the thin metal and flipping it up with the force of a thousand strong men trying to save a litter of puppies trapped under a burning car.

Christmas. The five individual tabs, stripped out into the approximate size and shape of the part of the key you stick in a door. Each individual tab has a tiny image of hand raised, fingers bent slightly inward, a keyhole filling the expanse of the empty palm. Something for your mind. Break one tab off at the perforated edge and drop it in my friend's extended hand.

"Thanks, man," he says, placing it under his tongue, saliva melting the trip off the paper. I stare at the repeating quartet for a moment more, wondering how I hadn't noticed the image before.

Break off another square and lick it up onto the very tip, extended out, catching that first snowflake of winter. Forecast calls for a white out. The tiny piece of paper sits there, resting, doing all the work through osmosis. While I just wait.

I imagine color literally draining from the image. The hand melting away, keyhole closing and opening up inside my mind, a transference. Literal becoming figurative, unlocking what?, is yet to be seen. Ha! As if the drug part of the product is actually contained in the ink. Preposterous.

I swallow. We wait. Sitting in silence, tapping our feet with the far-off beat. Like we don't want to break the spell or speak too soon and scare the acid away. Skittish dog without a collar running through traffic. I lift up the cooler and fish around the resting bucket of water—all of the ice going the way of the polar caps, disintegrating into nothing until we as a planet have nothing to show for ourselves.

I offer a cold brew (not cold brew the coffee variant, but beer, shorthand, vernacular) to Micah. He accepts wordlessly, letting product and extension of arm be the one with the purchasing power. I fish for another, cracking the seal as soon as I'm able to pass it to myself.

We sip. SLRRRRP. Coldish—enough—beer running down throats, easing anxiety as best as they know how. But it doesn't really work and feet tap not to a beat but to time ticking by.

Hmmm. I know something that could ease my anxiety, the bag of ketamine absentmindedly finding itself out of my pocket and opened as if by habit. Like a little spoonful will make all my troubles go away. Let the trip come on without worrying about it.

Do I have a problem? Am I developing micro-dependence? A-D-D-I-C-T-E-D. Buy an ounce off the hook up and use it just to make it through the day until I'm nothing but the product that defines me. I know they use ketamine nasal spray as a stop gap for those transitioning between antidepressants. But I'm not on any. Is this a self-medicating sort of SSRI situation?

Or, I can look at the other side of the coin. A watched pot never boils. Bound to spin myself out because I'm second guessing whether or not I'm tripping yet. I could just take this little bumpski, get my day started, and be gone with all this over-consideration that's only getting worse and worse by the moment.

Is this how people have drug freak-outs? Overthinking to the point of internal combustion. Bursting into flames just by considering it. Flame on. Jump off the side of a building because you can't handle the anxiety, not the high.

Like a savior, an angel coming down from the heavens and landing on the front porch of a house (that I don't own (I rent—I mean in this ecronomony)), beckoning me to join him in the afterlife: all my problems to be taken care of. Micah says, "let me get a bump."

Ah yes, just what I needed to hear. The echo chamber of exactly what I wanted standing straight, saluting, and reporting for duty.

"Sir, yes, sir!" I toss the bag over and he reaches for the chain around his neck. Feelin' froggy. "Wait," I say. "Take mine." I fish into my pocket and gently hand him the Rhinestone 24K gem I've come to call Dolly Parton.

Micah looks over my prized possession, impressed. Sun glinting off the rhines and flashing him in the eyes. This is some music-video shit. If tiny spoons starred in rap music videos flossing and acting bossy in fish-eyed lenses. A Hype Williams production. Put your spoons where my eyes can see. Krumping. Bumping.

"Oh damn, where'd you get this?" Micah asks, turning it over in his hands and respecting the craftsmanship, as a bit of a craftsman himself.

"Manifested it into existence." I say. He nods, understanding. Unimaginable beings sitting on shoulders making things happen whether we want them or not. Open up your mind and let the k-hole in.

Good friends don't ask questions. They let the moment breathe. Be the goon you are alone, and your friends don't mind?—that's a keeper. Hold on and don't let go.

Micah drops Dolly into her bag and pulls out enough to get him properly off his rocker. He brings Ms. Parton to his nose and let's his hairs tickle her round bosom. The drugs shoot up like a pinball released into the wild, rolling down the hill. Oh shit, can somebody grab that? It's headed straight for that gutter. Please for the love of god, will somebody grab my pinball.

The bag returns to its rightful home: my hands, spoon attached to the bag like there's some velcro contraption keeping them together, when in fact they're just pressed together diligently, Micah careful to protect the precious commodities he's been respectfully granted access to. My man knows respect.

Smart move, Micah. Props for saving me from myself, I think, as I dig out my own anti-anxiety medication. Power to powdered prozac. Micah laughs as if I said that out loud. Just laughing to himself, I'm sure, but I repeat my thoughts verbally just in case. "Power to powdered prozac," I say.

"Yeah. You just said that," he adds, shaming me slightly, but also go ahead call my bullshit see if I care. I'm a bullshit master. Been talking nonsense for 116 pages and haven't even gotten a casual complaint. Checked my inbox and everything. Nada. Please email complaints directly to **support@roland.com**. If I were one for footnotes, say a MZD or DFW, I might put one here, saying that this is actually the email address to a digital-instrument company I share a name with. But I'm not, so I won't.

"You just said that." I respond parodically, aggressively, like an impression of a dude roid-raged out, getting in a verbal quip at the Venice lifting gym, even jutting out my quads to show how strong I am and how much I can bench press.

"You just said, you just said that."

Soon we're about fifteen layers deep telling each other that they just said, just said, just said, just said, just said that. Laughing the whole way home like Kevin Hart (or whoever's the top of the game when this is read. The year is 2047 and the #1 comedian is a lady named FART) doing stand up for the children, and as an audience they're giving it all they got because they want to make Kevin or FART feel good about themselves not because they actually think they're funny.

HaaHaahhh HAHAHHAHHAHAAHAHAHAHHAHA. Haaaahhhhh. HA HA HA. The laughs keep coming this Fall at 9/7 central on Fox. Two guys sitting in lawn chairs: riffing on substances. The kind of programming that would skyrocket me to the level of artist I know in my soul to be but have yet to manifest into existence outside of tweets about pre-packaged pastries. True potential.

"Okay," I say, slapping my thighs and leaping to my feet in one simultaneous motion that scares my friend, spilling small fragments of beer out of the can he's nursing. "Let's do something."

"Okay," he responds.

No suggestions? Fine. I'm in control.

Micah's chill, but he's possibly too chill. The amount he brings to the idea table is somewhere between none at all and insignificant. He doesn't need to ask what, because the firmness with which he okayed my notion was clear as day that I've got to pick.

117

I've got no idea, but I fake like I do anyways, extending my hand for his. "Let's adventure." Micah takes it and I pull.

A little too hard. I fall back on my ass and take Micah with me. Chair collapsing underneath. Micah lands on me and we crack up, laughing so hard we can't do anything ever again for the rest of our lives but laugh. I'm sure it's fucking hysterical. American's Funnest Home Vidiots.

He pushes himself off me and rises to his feet with support from the collapsed camping chair. I hop to mine like I'm a cat and I just jumped off a building and I always land on my feet. Though that would discount all of the moments before when I was on my ass. But let's just forget about that for a brief second.

Life check: Wallet. Cellphone. Drugs. Spoon. I verbalize this and Micah pats pockets. Testicles, spectacles, wallet and watch. And we're off. Off to see the whatever. The wonderful whatever of whatever. Micah and I link arms and skip off through the tents, representing the scarecrow more than all the other major players: if I only had a brain.

§

Falafel. We both order it. Ending up at the food court (of all places!) with eight balls of ground chickpeas and two whopping spoonfuls of hummus sandwiched between enough triangles of pita to take down a tree, if pita were made of paper which I don't think it is.

We probably could have ordered one and split it, but that's not where our heads were at when we stepped to the counter at a complete loss of words outside of 'falafel please'—never forget please and thank you, no matter how high you are.

We sit on the grass approximately ten yards away from the truck. Aptly named FaLaLaLafel. Open up the styrofoam and start digging in, mouthfuls of food shoveled in without a care.

Behind us, a small eked out 'hello' comes begging through the microphone. Beauty Collective are smart to position food next to their workshop/meditation/yoga stage. This way as you're scarfing down grub, you can also better your mind, body and soul. Total rejuvenation package.

Micah doesn't even bother to look up, but I do because I'm a better person than him, and if somebody ekes out a hello, it's our responsibility on this planet of ours to acknowledge them with a hello back. I mean, it's the least you can do.

119

So I toss one out: "hurhhho," mouth full of that which makes my taste buds and stomach happy, searching the skyline of people for the place from where the noise came. I know the stage is in there somewhere, but it's blocked by people crossing and talking and generally getting their day started. The beautiful people who hardly ever eat, stopping for only enough to get them through the day, catching up with friends instead of proteins. Nice to see you. Did you have fun last night?

There she stands. Noname. Onstage. Have to look between two tall red-haired men, gigantic ginger vikings with matching beards (one long, one short). I want to say that the person behind them is what is important, but honestly, with a sighting that rare you take what you get. Basically two bigfoots chatting instead of communicating telepathically over long distances. Post it on the internet.

"Hello," she starts up again and I zoom past them and into full attention mode. "We're going to get started with Yoga here in about five minutes." Well, distracted attention: the trees shake behind her head, and I'm drawn to them, looking up at the branches taking on a life of their own, leaves billowing in the wind, like how do they even do that? What is the natural order of things to create such beauty? I laugh.

I look to Micah. He's staring at the food on his plate, drawing the Fibonacci sequence in the remaining hummus. He looks back at me. Hnh. His eyes are wide with wonder.

"You're high, man," he says. I laugh. Agreeing with him, but not appreciating the judgmental tone, even though there wasn't so much judgment in the tone as there was in the statement. Sure, it was a fact, but why you gotta be so upfront about it.

"You're high." I respond. Shows him.

"Most definitely." He repeats the phrase trying on different pronunciations. "mOHst DEFinitely. MOStt defINITley." We settle on Moist Dolphin. Aren't they all?, somebody behind us responds. We try to catch their gaze, but either they're so uninvested in their own punchline that they didn't even bother, or it is all just one big coincidence. Eether IIther.

I nudge Micah with the connective parts of my lower and upper arm, gesturing to the girl nervously pacing on stage.

That's her. *That her?* Yeah, that's her. *Okay, do something about it.* Now? *No time like the present or shit or get off the pot or some third familiar phrase that means hop to it yeehaw.* I don't know. *Come on, we've gone over this already.* Uhhh I'm terrible at yoga, operating at about a zero on the general stretchability scale. *You going to just run away?* Maybe. *What if you never see her again?* Everything's vibrating, man. *So?* I don't really know if I'm capable of a real conversation. *Not with that attitude.* You gonna run away with me or what? *Fine, let me just finish my Falafel.*

Micah pops one in his mouth and scoops up both our piles of trash. We lift ourselves up and throw the garbage where it belongs—making sure to separate out compost, recycling and just general swill—like good boys who care about the environment and are somewhere between fully and partially aware that the polar ice caps are melting, but have no clue what's going on with the Amazon.

Mid-stride, exit plan in motion and the second I hear her speak again, I stop frozen in my tracks. Leg up, stuck in the air until someone is able to thaw me out with a blowdryer. Micah

121

bumps into me from behind, causing my exaggerated pose to fall back down to Earth.

"Thank you everybody for getting up early for a little Yoga and meditation. Hope nobody is still awake from last night, but power to you if you are." Men and women spread out into their own private stretching space. It's as if they know exactly the length of their body and how far they can possibly push themselves without touching the other bodies around them.

Many step on yoga mats, unfurling cushioned sheets to hold some of their pressure of their body in down dog or another yoga pose that I've probably heard of but forgotten. Micah pats me on the back and releases me from the loyalty of company, exiting stage left (literally and figuratively all the world's a stage). I slowly lower myself to the ground and watch.

"My name is Aurora, I'll be your tour guide to the cosmos.[1] Don't worry, I know everybody's hurting after partying last night. I'll go easy on you." She laughs. They all follow suit.

Aurora. Aurora. Aurora. Aurora. Aurora.[2] I repeat it so as not to forget it. Aurora. Aurora. She LOOKS like an Aurora. I should have known this intuitively and not been calling her Noname like some guy that doesn't have telepathy, when I am in fact a guy who does have telepathy. Aurora delivers some heartfelt message to initiate the yoga. It's about the self, growth, resetting, restoring, deserving, and healing. Essentially the same spiel that every yoga teacher this side of the San Andreas fault delivers.[3]

----

1   Wittels, Harris. *Analyze Phish*, Earwolf.
2   Aurora
3   I'm sure it was better, but I'm more caught up in the experience than actually listening. Like that song "Listen to the Music," which is about someone at a concert who won't shut the fuck up and the narrator gently makes a suggestion that they actually listen, be in the moment, instead of being so caught up in themselves.

Normally, this rehashed screenplay[4] of every yoga teacher ever
bothers me, but today it doesn't. Maybe because it's coming
from the most beautiful face I've ever seen and I'm watching
more than listening.[5]

She gives people directions and they follow: close eyes, arms
to the sky, child's pose, stretch, all fours, tuck toes underneath,
lift knees, press hips towards the sky, extend legs, walk it out,
bend knee, press opposite heel, downward dog, breathe, inhale,
exhale, feel, round spine into plank, drop knees then chest then
chin to ground, release, lift into baby cobra, squeeze shoulders
together, open heart, release, press up to knees, tuck toes,
downward dog, hold, deep breath, bend knees, exhale, take
steps to the edge of the mat, grab opposite elbows, ragdoll—
forward fold, swing side to side, loosen, releasing tension, roll
up holding on to elbows, lift up through chest, inhale, exhale,
higher to the sky, breathe, exhale, center, inhale, sun salutation,
exhale, forward fold, inhale, lengthen, exhale, step right leg all
the way back, drop knee to floor, inhale, reach both arms all the
way up, low lunge, exhale, hands down, lift back knee, step into
plank, knees, chest, chin to mat, extend forward, baby cobra,
release, turn over to left side, press right foot to floor, lift pelvis
up, right arm to the sky, into wild thing, make my heart sing,
make everything groovy, open through chest, release, turn over
to belly, baby cobra, higher, up to knees, child's pose, breathe,
exhale, come forward, tuck toes, downward facing dog, step to

---

4   Final Draft CCXX available now
5   Oh shit, I already covered this in footnote number 4. I'm just repeating
myself now, caught in an endless loop of nonsense, huh? Good thing nobody reads
the footnotes. Honestly, I read the entirety of *Infinite Jest* without them and I feel like
I got it just fine. Everybody says otherwise, but fuck everybody. We all consume art in
our own special way, you know? And if I don't wanna read the way I'm supposed to,
well then, that's my prerogative. This is America. You know I'm not saying that our
freedoms are limited. Because as a country we've progressed socially a lot further than
at any point in the past. But what I am saying is that it's a person's right to choose. I
guess the major question I'm left with is, do you even remember that earlier I made a
comment about not being a footnote writer? Or was this spread for naught?

the front of the mat, inhale, lengthen, exhale, fold, inhale, roll
self up to standing, stand, stand in the place where you work,
now face west, think about direction, wonder why you haven't
before, exhale, inhale, reach arms up to the sky, exhale, hands
to heart, take a moment for self, reach arms up to the sky,
exhale, forward fold, inhale, lengthen through spine, exhale,
step left foot to the back of the mat, reach both arms up, low
lunge, open self up, square hips, release hands, tuck toes, lift
knee, plank, knees chest chin down, slide forward, release toes,
baby cobra, attack, hold, inhale, exhale, bend left knee, roll
onto right side, press foot to the mat, ground, flex, lift body
up as high as possible, higher baby, left arm reach up and over,
release tension, release position, roll over to belly, hands to
side of body, baby cobra, release, press self up to knees, child's
pose, deep inhalation into lungs, exhale, let go all that no
longer serves, let go of negativity, let go of stress, welcome
this pleasant moment, welcome this breath, welcome self-love,
acceptance, patience, roll over to knees, downward facing dog,
deep breath, walk feet forward, forward fold, grab opposite
elbows, relax, sway, be loose, release hands, inhale, lengthen
through spine, exhale, take arms behind back, lace fingers,
extend, hold, lower, allow hands to come to front of mat,
deep breath, exhale, inhale, long exhale, feel stretch through
shoulders, let go, lift halfway, standing, hands behind back
open through chest into gentle backbend, inhale, exhale, back
to center, stand at the top of mat, inhale, lengthen, exhale,
fold, inhale, reach arms up to the sky, exhale, hands to heart,
feel energy within, inhale, bend knees, step left foot back
behind front knee, arms up, warrior 1, shoulders square, deep
breath, exhale, extend front knee, hands to hip, grab opposite
elbows, pyramid pose, feel body responding to posture, push
and pull hips back and forward, feel the release of tension,
breathe deeply, inhale, exhale, lift back heel, bend front knee,
step back, crescent lunge, arms up, inhale, arms down, exhale,

step back, plank, knees to floor, elbows chest and chin, slide forward, inhale, cobra, higher, engage muscles, release, press up to knees, child's pose, round out spine, keep eyes closed, bring awareness back into internal awareness, self into present moment, come onto knees, tuck toes, downward dog, walk to front of mat, bend knees, sit in center, extend legs, seated head to toe forward fold, inhale, reach arms to the sky, reach toward ankles, close eyes, awareness to breath, deeper, sink into the ground, exhale, give body permission to surrender, let go of worries, breathe, release, hands behind back, scoot forward, release into savasana, know what savasana is, relax, palms open to sky, close eyes, take a deep breath, exhale, let go, relax, surrender, release body into mat, feel heart beating in chest, remind self of beautiful existence, notice heaviness of body, inhale, welcome gratitude, exhale, visualize self in control of circumstances and reactions in life, deep breath, exhale, bring awareness to body, reach arms over head, stretch, take a moment to find center, close eyes, open palms up to the sky, inhale, reach arms up to the sky, exhale, bring hands to heart, bow down to heart, thank self.

"Namaste."
"Namaste," all of the practitioners repeat back, refreshed, revitalized, and ready to take on the day. Maybe I should have participated instead of staring entranced at bodies bending in ways earnestly impressive to me. Sure, the view is nice, but—

It's more than that. Pure athleticism. A ballet dancer completing a fourteen-point turn, a basketball player absolutely dominating the boards with no one able to catch up, nailing the 7/10 split in the final frame of a bowling tournament. Can't even begin to imagine how half-way decent about myself I'd feel if I'd taken the initiative to even attempt a third of the 290 separate directions given.

As people begin to fade away back to campsites or dance floors, I spot Aurora hopping off the stage, toweling her face off with a purple hand towel. The sweat beading on her face glistens and sparkles, shining out and bright, bouncing off the beauty of the sun and reflecting it for all the world to see.

Bent over, rolling up her mat in the grass, I quickly weave through those lounging (or eating) between she and me.

"Yoga, huh?" I ask. She laughs without even looking up, finishing the complicated task of rolling a flat mat into a cylindrical tube. It's challenging and requires deep focus. None of this patronizing question bullshit. I love that laugh though. I'd challenge men a million times stronger than me just to hear her chuckle. I'd sit through 4000 yoga classes just at the hope of a giggle dropped in the final one.

When she rises up to see who had the dumb comment, the kind of comment that would get nothing but disgusted disinterest in her hometown of Los Angeles or Santa Barbara or San Luis Obispo or—her eyes brighten with excitement instead.

"You!" she says, instilling nothing but pure and bright and good faith in me that the universe is in my favor and she doesn't hate me like I thought she might after my shameful disappearing act.

"Me!" I reply, matching energy. We stand there for a moment shuffling feet like kids in the school yard after just figuring out what sex is, and thinking about what's behind that dress or underneath those shorts. Curious, but nervous.

"Aurora."

"Roland."

"Roland, I'm headed back to my camp. Walk with me." Aurora gestures with her head in the complete and total opposite way of my campsite—as if we were destined to meet despite the directional difference of our home bases. With a nod, she kicks off and I follow. Puppy dog, sure maybe a little bit. I don't care.

"What the hell happened to you last night?" she asks.
"K-hole," I respond. She laughs. That laugh. I FUCKING LOVE IT. Any and all laughter please come this way. Infectious like SARS ripping through 2003 China or the plague in 1347 or—I laugh back, in on the joke. The joke that is taking too much drugs. Punchline, me.

"I thought you were mad at me."
"No, no. Just stupid." Another laugh, smaller, but scratches the itch.
"Been there."

We settle into stride, weaving through crowds of bubbling energy. The whole party is on a good one and we're swimming upstream, matching their vibe with the ether between us singeing fire red hot and burning. The opposite of those headed to the stage to get their first taste of (full) sound for the day. Passing between us could cause an electrical shock that one might never truly recover from.

"So what's your plan today?" she asks, with genuine interest. As if there wasn't only one thing to do: head to the stage and dance dance dance until the sun comes up and then some. Love Language is why we're all here after all, right? For what he regularly refers to as his 'best set of the year.' Superstar DJ, here we go.

"I mean. Love Language, right?"
"Totally. TimeCop too.
"Totally TimeCop and love Love Language."
"That's a trip."

Sharing in the simplicity of sentences, not mattering whether they matter or not. Playful, but she feels it too. Not just me writing the narrative in my head. There is no fast forwarding but pause. Two small rectangles hanging on the freeze frame hoping this moment can stay...

"I could trip." She adds to the conversation out of nowhere. Unsuggested except through my mind. Mind control. You're getting sleepy. "It's been a couple of months but I'm ready to open the door back out to space. Too long since I've been a molecule."

I grab her (gently, come on I'm a gentleman) by the forearm and pull her off the trail. We cross over two men dressed like tweedle dee and tweedle dum—if they wore all black and neon '90s JNCOs industrial warehouse tracksuit fashion—into a jungle-gym style dome set up with carpet and pillows. A lounge for all that desire it. At this time of day with the sun attacking one side, and military grade industrial shade cloth not quite doing the trick, this safe haven is relatively empty.

We drop to our asses and bounce a moment on the soft pillows, floating on the air that is comfort and bedding. I dig into the pocket and hand her the two bags plus spoon. Purple, ketamine. "Hold these I say." She does. No questions asked. I quickly unfold the remaining three strips of LSD, and in breaking one off, extend it to her, my hand in the same position as the one on the tab.

She quickly grabs the square and pops it in her mouth like a starving server recovering a french fry left abandoned on a table by someone who always orders more than they need.

An excitement in her eyes, pupils dilating before my very eyes. As if the release of endorphins just at the mere mention got her instantly high. Dope. My kind of girl. I consider the last two tabs in my palm.

Here, I am, an hour or so in. I feel it but I'm not tripping the life fantastic: unable to stand, trees melting into visions of unreality, making connections to the cosmos that teach me the way of the warrior and total truth. On my rocker. What could it hurt to double dip? So I do, taking the second and third tab and adding them to my tab, doubly.

Aurora asks if she can hit these (referring to the bags in her hands. My drugs. Our drugs?) and I say something like oh of course do them all if you want to, what's yours is mine—what's that phrase in spanish again? Casa. Casa. Casa.

"Exciting," Aurora says, rubbing her hands together, excitedly, before digging the spoon softly, daintily, into each of the bags. The gentle touch that only a woman could have. Not us men with our bear paws and piss-poor reaction time. Shove hand into beehive to get honey now. We make house work. Build empires. Collapse societies. She takes tiny bumps out of each bag, sussing out which one is which and appropriately deciding how much more to take of the which which she'd rather which about.

Woah, shit. The words woah and shit repeat in my head, not out of fear, but out of woah. Literally an image of the words 'woah' and 'shit' fill in the space around me and Aurora, fading in and out of existence, turning over into three-dimensions. I pop a woah like a bubble and shits fill in its place. I turn the shit over and reverse it: tihs. This is ridiculous and I shoo it away. Clean vision. That's more like it. Purple Ketamine I tell her.

Aurora grabs my arm and places four bags and two spoons inside my hand. She shuts my fingers around the drugs and quotes the Lord of the Rings to me: "Keep it secret. Keep it safe." I do, shoving the bags haphazardly into my pocket. Back in the honey pot.

Now it's her turn to grab my forearm, and she does after standing up in the kind of smooth motion that only a yoga instructor would be capable of. Not my crickety old bones. Haven't stretched since the Civil War (2006-2007, Marvel Comics). But she gets me to my feet, no problem at all and drags me through the festival grounds like I'm a toddler who got in trouble for hiding in clothing racks at the mall, and now I'm being rushed out to the car and driven home in silence, except replacing anger with giddy joy.

We take back paths, alleyways, hopping over generators and behind official looking tents where business happens—home base for the build team, medic, production crew—and pop out behind the DJ booth. A small conclave of people groove behind the decks. Whoever's spinning, has everybody blissed out, arms up, waving to nothing, operating much the same way seaweed tries to touch the sky from the bottom of the ocean.

"Come on," she says, pulling me up on the platform, backstage. "Bird Song is a friend of mine." We join in with the seaweed people. Bird Song twists knobs and hits buttons, making minute changes that I can't begin to perceive. Wonder if it's plugged in at all except from my vantage point behind his bobbing head the lights on the CDJs and Mixing Board pop, alive. Technology, bright reds and greens and oranges and yellows showing how the music works if you know how to read this kind of computer language.

I don't, so my fascination with techno's technology wanes as quickly as it comes and I move my eyes out and over the edge of the booth, a swarm of people crowding the man in a tiny vest and a little fez hat, asking for his attention, begging for it with their dance moves, competing to see who is the ultimate dancer.

Look at me Mr. DJ, I'm dancing the hardest for you. Me! Me! I'm the one! Their faces are hilarious, contorted and twisted, one eye switching places with the other eye, tongues out like Michael Jordan on the slam dunk.

This is I guess where I should have some sort of bio breakdown for the DJ. Shooting average. RBI. Pizza Boxes Folded per Hour. That kind of thing. But all I really know is that Bird Song is just one of the guys. Been around since Festivalia had its first major iteration but isn't particularly of note. We're just here. We're the noteworthy party.

Aurora grabs me by the sleeve and pulls my 6'5" ear down to her 5'7" mouth. Volume too loud for me to hear without her yelling which would be majorly uncouth considering our active participation in the music. Providing background support, energy.

Backstage, the lot of us around the DJ, are like a cast of extras that fill out the scene on a major Hollywood blockbuster. You

131

don't notice them until they're overacting and then there's embarrassing YouTube compilations edited together of them. People of Boiler Room.

"He's my next-door neighbor!" She tells me. I don't care but I don't tell her that.
"Rad!"

There is a culture at Beauty Collective of knowing the DJs the most. They're supposedly down to Earth guys, giving off the vibe that they are easy to get to know. I've never tried. But that don't mean I don't have respect for those who do. Who wouldn't want to be friends with the guys responsible for starting a cultural movement? 500,000 social media fans can't be wrong. That's some next level friendship right there.

We nudge in closer, squeezing out the riff raff between us and the DJ. Next in line for autographs, we're the #1 dancers. Suck it, everybody else.

Do I pay attention to the twists and turns that weave us through an orchestral maneuver of house tunes? Not in the least. It's all fun and games until you're in the DJ booth with a beautiful face and that face keeps moving and it takes everything in your power, the universe pulsating forcefully around you, trying desperately, to hold onto that visage. I'm not about to lose her again. Not now, not while I have her in my grasp, tripping on the same supply. Kismet.

～

After the set, our backs back in the grass, the exact spot we first met. Instead of stars we watch as clouds move ever-so-slightly across the dome holding us in, pressurized, hints of color in the sky. Floral hues passing over gradients of blue. The moment I stop taking all five senses for granted. The mere thought of not having one is so far beyond the realm of imagination, yet staring me in the face, that maybe I haven't been fully realizing the power of vision this entire time.

"I feel squirrely," she says, rolling off her back and onto her side, staring at the place where my eyes would be if I would only roll over and stare back.

"Yeah, that makes sense," I respond, offering no further connection to the man named Squirrel whose little paws were all over this stuff. Acid is full of synchronicities. Harping on every single one would be a book within itself. I turn to my side and we link eyes. The curve of her smile peeks out between strands of hair crossing her face. We blink simultaneously.

"Okay," she responds to the lapse in time, long enough for me to have made a move if I was going to. "Let's do something." She's up and onto her feet in a series of four quick movements. I think it takes me somewhere around seventeen. Once we're both standing—a real courtesy on her part to wait—she takes my hand and starts running to nowhere.

"Where are we going?," I ask, between huffed breaths.

She laughs. It inspires so much joy in my heart that I understand what it must be like for blood to pump through the heart. This is purpose. Moist dolphin. Imagine two mannequins on treadmills, posed in all their festival best. Mid-stride. But the store-design specialist got a little too playful with the Roland and Aurora mannequins. While their arms are linked and their bodies are normal, their smiles are two to four sizes too large for their faces, the curl of their lips extending well past the frame of their jowls.

We continue the back way, down a path I would have never known existed if I weren't temporarily operating as one of the cool kids. A trail of wires, connecting power to generators, that we follow to a part of artist camping that feels VIP and exclusive and not meant for normal eyes.

Sequestered off by a magical set of trees that had seemingly hidden it completely from view, we come upon nine or ten different (who's counting) automobiles situated in a perfect circle. Like the old timey wagon train, blocking out buffalo herds of inquisitive ravers and prying eyes. Above the vehicles, a thin, tautly pulled piece of shade cloth keeps a common area protected from invasive sunlight.

She stops, eyes bright, arms raised to the sky, a prize model on a game show. "My home!"

While Hampton certainly had things figured out—drug money buying him a van that perpetuated the sale of more drugs—this part of the campsite looked about as run-down as it did impressive. Money couldn't buy this kind of caravan commune. This was tender, love and care.

Calling these automobiles is unfair, because they are more than that. They are homes—fully formed places of residence. Trailer Hitch RVs, Tiny Homes, Airstreams, Teardrop Campers—decked out with the kind of personal effects that scream I OWN THIS AND I DIDNT JUST RENT IT TO BE COMFORTABLE AT THE FESTIVAL FOR THE WEEKEND.

Aurora pulls me between vehicle-homes and into the center of their personal vortex. A small child in diapers runs underneath two dreadlocked men who intensely consider their next four moves over a game of chess, while a grandmotherly figure lets the blender whirl whipping up a batch of margaritas. A game of cornhole erupts in applause as one team sinks their dusted bag perfectly into the open hole of the other side's wooden platform.

I want to ask if they live this way every day, but I know the answer. This is the other side of things. Those who live the festival life and aren't just tourists one weekend at a time. 5-9, not 9-5. It's always been somewhat of an appealing prospect, drop it all and come what may, but like, how do you pay your cellphone bill? What do you do when you have to shit?

She pulls me over to a painted pink airstream trailer, teardrop shaped and hitched to the back of a matching pink pick-up truck. Potted succulents in a box hanging out of—what I can only assume is—-the bedroom window. Aurora tells me that she bought it off a dude in Joshua Tree after she inherited a bit of money.

135

I get some approximation of her life story and must regurgitate it for fear of forgetting it when my brain is right again, repeating each detail in the internal monologue as she says them out loud. She met these people at a regional Burn in Southern Colorado after running away from a bad situation at home. While she hasn't been to Burning Man yet, this was going to be 'her year.' They live by "Burning Man's Ten Principles," which she repeats for me even though I've heard them a number of times before, albeit from far less lovely of a source. "Radical Inclusion, Gifting, De-Commodification, Radical Self-Reliance, Radical Self-Expression, Communal Effort, Civic Responsibility, Leave No Trace, Participation, and Immediacy." These phrases get tossed around regularly at your average camping music festival, so I am familiar enough with the not-so radical radical concepts. Their caravan is constantly moving, living truly off the grid—the word grid repeats in my mind, in a grid nonetheless—helping each other survive against the desert's beautiful brutality.

"Cool," I eventually mutter when it seems like she is finished. What did I just say? Did I say cool to the history of her existence? I say it again. Four letters, not a curse word. Cool.

"K?," I add, hoping she agrees and we can break this cycle of awkward authenticity with some substance abuse. She agrees. We take a seat on a green oversized bean-bag chair that has the words cum and fort spray-painted on each side. We share spoons—one for her and one for me, before melting into the bean-filled bag of shared assurances.

Ket, can exist as this middle ground to normalize oneself back (at least into a chemical compound), for a brief fucking second. When LSD wants to take you off shooting against the stars a little bit of K anchors you to the spaceship. Hold on for your life dear, this is gonna be bumpy as all hell, but we're gonna make it through.

Aurora rolls off the cushion and onto a dusty carpet that looks like it's seen decades of desert abuse. Wind-battered, color-faded, dirt-encrusted, but she pats the spot next to her like the most comfortable place on Earth. I do as I'm told, climb off after her and take a seat exactly where her hand used to be. She flips her body around and lines her spine up directly with mine. Full support, lean back.

Wriggling in her seat, we simultaneously give back massages to ourselves and to each other, using our spines instead of hands chopping and screwing along the plates, leaving one person to do all the work and the other to reap all the benefits.

"Feels good, right?" she asks.

"Uh huh," I respond, not having felt this good in who can remember how long. I feel my cock stiffen, adding a sexual element to something that could be left otherwise completely platonic. But we writhe in unison, back and forth, side to side, like a great fuck where you're both so deeply in sync it really gives meaning to the phrase two to tango. Backs instead of fronts creating a unity between people that doesn't involve genital insertion.

Aurora leans forward to touch her toes and in the process separates our backs. This stretch, that I'm in no way able to take part in, turns into a somersault, and our connection is broken.

A tingle rises up my back, strong like it could support a five-story apartment complex. They say that acid stores itself in your spine, and while I've never been so sure about that, whatever we just took part in seemed to activate an internal light that spreads to every quarter inch of me. From fingertips to cerebral cortex.

"The cosmic joke is that we all just want someone to rub our backs. But I'm looking for someone to rub backs with," Aurora long ago figuring out what it'll take the rest of us a lifetime to come to terms with.

Maybe it's just all the years of acid being reactivated in my spine, hello buddy, remove yourself from any normal sense of societal care, because we're on our own groove here, but I move in for a kiss. Our lips intertwine with the same cohesive sense of unspoken movement, tongues twirling in complete disregard for anything but each other. Her hand on my thigh, and mine at her side, both massaging in circles, vibrations surging through our bodies like only acid can, hoping for this moment to last forever.

∽

Lips pull away from mine, and while my eyes stay closed I can feel the world around us changing. A looming presence watching over us like a hawk coming down to snatch a chihuahua left out too long in a Palm Springs backyard. Eyes open to reveal a man standing over us. Hand on Aurora's head, the man squats down to our level.

"Hello, friend," he says with the sort of ominous overtones that tell me he's not actually calling me his friend. Delivery short and uninviting, he extends a hand. "I'm Dr. Mongoose, pleased to make your acquaintance."

I readjust to see a man, who's energy offered a much different presence yesterday. Entirely. The man who told me I could conjure up anything if I just believed it to be so, scowls after his truth magic has come to fruition on my behalf.

"Larry!" Aurora squeals, leaping onto the older man, putting her arms around his neck, and killing the tension in the open-air living room. I back up, letting them have their space. She kisses him on both cheeks, so happy to see him that I'm having trouble configuring what this relationship dynamic could be.

Once she rolls off, and lets the man breathe his own air again, he asks how her yoga class went. Completely ignoring me, they speak as if I've never even existed. Blah blah blah.

A momentary glance from this man's side eye instills in me a sudden fear that he has chosen to imagine me out of existence. If Dr. Larry Mongoose, with his graying hair and incredible stage presence, were just to imagine me away—poof I'd be gone, back to my campsite or never even alive to begin with. Feel myself fading away, skin turning translucent and the brain shutting down like a factory assembly line at 5:01. Union guys come in and flip the switch, taking a minute for everything to settle into sedentary, but it will get there.

For some reason I can't shake this notion and I'm unable to listen to the words coming out of their mouths as they smile and nod and counter and hold hands and stare right through me like I've never been here at all.

"Oh!" Aurora says loudly, pulling my soul back into my body and really feeling the grass underneath my palms. "This is Roland."

Dr. Mongoose feigns surprise, head-turn, hand to chin, opening his eyes wide as if he really had forgotten I was here. His intense gaze narrows, bearing into me with hypnotic suggestion, the iris expanding at will, inviting me to come inside. Not sure I want to.

"Yes, yes, you were there at my talk, right?" The ego is a fragile beast that has those who have it grasping to hold onto it. After letting the momentary pause fill in for the lapse in conversation, he adds, "So Roland, what do you think we are? Real or Imaginary?"

That's a good question. I sure thought about it, but don't know if I ended up coming to any kind of comprehensive conclusion. I look to Aurora, wondering what her take might be, but she's lost in adoration and no hope to me now. Maybe I am not real. Nor his highness neither. It's all just part of the illusion. Puppet master pulling the strings even if they're wonky. Yes, master.

I start to sweat. It's hot out, I think, despite being covered by shade and this sweat, dripping down my face cold, feeling flu-like.

He continues prattling—maybe he's the only one who really exists and we're all just figments of his making—digging me a hole deeper and deeper that I'm not sure I can get out from. I feel my brain turn off through my stomach, processing that he is the wrong kind of person to be caught in a conversation with on a head full of LySergic aciD diethylamide.

Dr. Mongoose's eyes look into mine, mind intruding into mine. "Though I'm not sure how helpful the three hits of LSD coursing through your brain are going to be in answering that." Though his lips no longer move, I hear him say the phrase: *bad trip*.

He laughs; she laughs; I laugh.

I can feel every fiber of my being vibrating—or is that quivering?—eons of isotopes each on their own very special hum, separating out the parts of my body meant to be held together. My mind is over in Sri Lanka while my hands and feet each take residence in one of the Dakotas and Carolinas. My dick is here, but that's inconvenient because my balls are back over at my tent.

We spin. By we I mean the muscles and organs that are no longer in control of their fate. Sphincter pulsates, puckering up for a kiss, but really about to lose control and drop unpleasantness all over the Serbian rug hovering beneath our feet. A full force reality check in the very inopportune.

A pitter-patter of music starts to play from a small set of speakers nearby. One that can't possibly begin to compete with the big boys over yonder, but manages to take control of our microcosm of a beat scene nonetheless. Renegade raving. Bird Song has taken to a set of campsite CDJS, slowly building a song into the natural flow of conversation. Good vibing and getting down, the people around us start to move to their own personal dance floor.

Aurora leaps to her feet before helping me to mine. "Bird Song secret set!," she shouts with the excitement of someone experiencing it for the first time and not what must be a regular occurrence being neighbors and all. But I guess that joie-de-vivre is part of what makes life worth living.

The shift in weight to my feet would be best described as unsettling. My head feels like it weighs upwards of 100 pounds, dragging ass back to the soft pillows that pepper the landscape. My sneakers glued to the ground. I'll just stay here, thanks, with the inconsiderate gum chewers of America leaving their ABC en masse for me to step upon, doing the work of gravity to keep me held to the ground while I'm on the brink of floating away. My body betrays, upwards of a hundred fuck yous.

I need to lie down. My head is swimming, but so is the air around me. Faces slip away into nothingness. Ether surging through the empty space of presence, overloading the matrix and coming back down right in front of me with a sneer and a smile. I close my eyes, but this doesn't make it any better. Try to swallow. I come up short there too. These hits really seems to be hitting hard, almost forgotten I'd taken them for a minute there. Fool I am. Bad at Drugs.

Aurora's face comes into focus, pulling me back into myself. If only for a moment. The background wiggles with the excitement of action, you've gone and done it this time Roland. "Are you okay?" Aurora asks a couple of times, but all I'm able to do is nod my head from side to side. The trails of whipping motion hold place across my vision, painting with all the different shades of purple and blue in those 120-color boxes of crayons. Aquamarine and Cerulean and Wisteria and Fuchsia.

Boof. Fall back into a seat like the legs don't work anymore or they never worked and all of a sudden the tendons give out, snap and break apart, an overused rubber band. How did I even get here? Wake up. Snap out of it.

I sit up straight and my back clicks into track. Spine realigning out of caveman and into neanderthal. Tiny fragmental remnants of hundreds of doses of LSD (yay me) swirling around in spinal fluid just waiting to be retriggered by some sight or sound or back alignment, man and woman finding their physical limitations with stretching exercises.

Flashbacks aren't meant to happen when you're already on a good one, but this feels layered. Old clouds sitting in front of new ones. Slightly off key. Red and blue colored lenses set marginally off from each other to give the sense of three dimensions on movie screens, but me and my mind hundreds of times over. CTRL+C CTRL+V CTRL+C CTRL+V.

Close my eyes and breathe in through the sockets. Meditative reaction to the terrifying is the only solution that I know works in any real measure. So I suck in air with intentionality and hold it in my lungs like how I'd been taught to smoke pot back in High School.

When I exhale, I consider the phrase anxiety being pushed out of my mouth. Neon gradient gif, drop-shadow and stroke, photoshopped graphic-design tools cycling through in my mind, pushing the word away as beautifully constructed as it is.

A-N-X-I-E-T-Y.

The letters nx keep becoming c's and ety, a d. The word shifting from anxiety to acid and back and forth like one of those pictures where if you look one way it's an old hag, and with a refreshed perspective, a beautiful lady. Toggling between one word I want and the other I don't, the blackness isn't filled with the woo-sah I need. The back of my eyelids betraying me in the way that only too much of a good thing can do.

Too high and I say so out loud. A supportive voice close to my face tells me that it's okay. I open my eyes again to see Aurora standing over me exuding the warmth of concern. Nothing less sexy than a man on too many drugs. Well—

Could rip off my clothes and run through the festival screaming about how money isn't even real if you think about it. Let the second hand click by and I'll be back to normal, but in this now, it doesn't feel that way.

I'm going to be high forever, at least that's what the demons in the back of my mind keep telling me. You're broken.

I'm broken. We're broken. Three tiny little demon heads spinning—they're MY demon heads now. Circling circling circling. Repetition Repetition Reptilian. Except the third repetition keeps autocorrecting to reptilian. I mean what's going on here? Look at those words, rounded letters. Circling. Hitting from all quadrants. Sixteen different separate boxes, it's like I get it. I get what a bug feels like.

A gentle touch on my shoulder. I can feel purple lines of Aurora—mountains majesty—pouring through hand and shoulder. My body fills with that energy, narrowly avoiding an empty husk of black as I picture myself without organs or water, but an outline of skin. Associated droning dulcet tones, a strikingly different speed than Bird Song's set superimposed and soundbleeding over the main festival speakers, calm me.

One eye opens and then the other. The brain can't process more than one bit of me at a time. We're back here in this caravan commune and not off in Jasper, Texas watching Ishmael Dick try and fail to cut acne off his face with a lucky razor blade named Artery.

Standing in front of me is the girl who I've been chasing my entire life. Her features transform between all of my past loves. Oscillating eyeballs and switching smiles between Eileen and Lauren and Jennifer and Aurora. All the girls I thought I've loved before.

Aurora's face settles into place. Sure the eyes still wriggle, but that's to be expected. What is she saying? Her words are lost in the music, dropping from her mouth and catching the wind, the bombastic speaker behind me stealing attention from all that is good and great and worth our time in the world.

145

I want to scream: "Shut up! Shut up! Stop the music," but more people have piled around the speakers. Dr. Mongoose has long since abandoned us, leading a conga line through the dance floor, stealing evil glances as he passes by. Aurora looks longingly at her people, having the time of their lives, while she runs her hand through my hair, soothing, calming.

The space around us fills in, and it's like *can't you people see I'm having a bad time?* Of course they can't. No room for bad vibes at the music festival. Shake 'em off to the beat and you'll be right as rain. Stuff down, ignore. Bottle. Don't acknowledge your problems at home. Forget about how you spend every fucking day sitting at a desk weighing what life would be like if you stopped posting nonsese about nosh but you can't even afford a cup of coffee from the stand down the street—the one the cute girl works at—how are you going to quit if you literally need the paycheck to survive. Become one of the free people you so desperately want to be.

This is proof that I can't hang. That I'm unlovable. She looks at me like the pathetic fuck I've known my entire life that I am. The word worthless swirls around my brain like the tail of soft serve.

"Can you stand?" She says to me, finally, sound connecting with my ears. Thank the god that doesn't exist. Or maybe he does. Or maybe I'm him. Or maybe we all are. Or maybe she's the LSD that's working her tricky magic on me. Gotta storm before you can be reborn.

I nod my head. The Little Engine that Could. The Little Roland that Should. I think I can, I think I can. With all my might I push my body forward and into her extended arms. She holds me like a mother would, child in outstretched arms, walking even if they don't know how.

Resting the majority of my weight on her shoulder, Aurora drags me directly through the spontaneous dance party and to her home sweet home, pink-airstream succulents calling out to me by name: "worthless, hey worthless. We don't even need water, but you'd still probably kill us."

Aurora unlatches the door and throws me inside. Her bed is made perfectly with a rainbow zebra bedspread. A girl who makes her bed in the morning even at a music festival, I swoon, and my whole body swoons too, collapsing to her bed in a way that nullifies the swoon. We're not going to end up happily ever after. Not after this. She repeats it's okay it's okay as if that's actually going to make me feel any better about this situation.

"Do you want some landing gear?" she asks.

Xanax. Yes. That'll knock me out, take the edge off, set me right as rain. Old reliable. Consistent transition out of reality. Make room for a break in the unending narrative dragging along in my head. If not my only way in and out of scenes. Sleep is for the weak.

Wake up refreshed, relaxed and ready to take on day four. What time is it? What does it matter? I nod my head. Aurora digs into a drawer and pulls out a prescription pill container. Child lock top off and she pours some into her hand.

"Whole bar, okay?" she asks. I nod again, yes. "This is going to knock you out." She smiles, reassuringly. What a sweetheart. Dump my ass once I'm able to get myself out of this.

Bar in mouth, followed by a swig from a water bottle. Ice cold sends the bar down my throat, off to do the work that pharmaceutical corporations make damn sure it's supposed to. The back of my eyelids become a safe space again. Words betraying my existence fade, replaced with the comforting lines and shapes of sacred geometry. The lines of the mathematically divine.

"Thank you," I mutter out, rolling over onto my back and looking up at her. She runs a hand through my hair. It's nice. The faraway look in her eyes maybe says otherwise.

"You get some rest, okay?" Aurora rises to her feet, and heads to the door. She pauses in the entry way for one final second. It's like that scene in a movie where someone has something to say, but they don't really know what to say, and both characters turn their backs, but they both secretly hope they'll turn forward, and they do, but at different times, so that thing never gets said.

We suffer in that unsaid thing. But we're also both really fucking high, so it's like, what even was that thing? Good luck? We're all counting on you?

The door shuts behind her and I return to the rotating, twisting, synchronized swimming shapes that play ad nauseum in the space of my mind. Like a really sick planetarium show. I wonder if it looks similar for everybody or if it's just me.

If you don't imagine beautiful pictures in your head, shut the fuck up.

§

12:07 AM. My phone reads this time from the top left-hand corner of the screen. The only light in relative darkness. Apps aren't vibrating off screen which tells me I'm on the other side of my drug dilemma. It still looks good though, letters popping off the screen, graphic design thumbs up emoji. You've got to be kidding me, whole teams putting in WORK to make this shit shine just like this.

Still high. Just not too high. Ideal. Back from the brink and ready to barty. Party, shit. Haha.

Fuck, what was that? I haven't tripped out that bad since I was sixteen and my mom caught me smoking weed. Got so high I thought I was going to die. The panic attack to end all panic attacks. Not now, then. Then was worse than now.

The best part about a bad trip is getting up, dusting off, and riding that skateboard again. You never learn if you don't fail.

I'm the definition of fail. In some girl's airstream trailer, while she's off at the rave, the headliner having started with minutes ticking by, me missing out on all the good stuff. Oh wait, I guess it's Monday, isn't it. Shit, let me start over...

MONDAY

Or is it technically still Sunday? That is the eternal question of music festivals. The one that we all keep asking and joking about. Do days start when they technically start?Do they start once awoken from slumber? Or are they only brought upon by the rise of the sun? Hmm...

If anybody were to subscribe to A or B, it would in fact be Sunday, but I'm more of a C kind of guy in that we need to strike-through that ~~MONDAY~~ and pretend it never happened.

SUNDAY (CONT'D)

Day's not over while the night's still happening. Sure, I missed a couple hours of the evening, but just because the clock struck midnight doesn't mean I'm Cinderella gonna turn back into a pumpkin. Nah, there's still night to be had. Let's go have it.

I open up the door and this once-bustling commune is deader than that shuttered suburban mall in every town this side of the 1980s. A ghost of a once-lively reminder of how people lived and played and spent their time.

The music from the stage feels a million miles away, like I've entered a portal out to the Joshua Tree Integratron and not still present here in our mountainous, chaparral climate. Love Language's midnight set passes through this pinhole of sound, muddled into nearly nothing as part of this nowhere place. Is this what silence is?

Shadows flicker with the wind, supplanted by neon strips, coming alive thanks to well-placed lanterns and anything in between. I pass through the shadows, contemplating becoming one, if I haven't already.

The second I step outside the border of these caravan walls, the sound comes through crystal clear, breaking the sound barrier like Chuck Yaeger entering and exiting my brain in the midst of a Wikipedia wormhole binge.

The chill settles in. I see the point of a wagon circle. Protected from the the buffalo but also from the cold. Hold warmth in rather than winds blustering about in shorts and a t-shirt. 95 to 59 in a matter of hours. Perfect opposites except that's not how things work in numerology. The great warming power of the sun is patently not on fleek.

I'm fucking bored of being serious. So deeply fucking bored. Sure, I had a harrowing hafternoon with hLSD, but that's not gonna set me back for the rest of my life. What's that saying? Uh, if you love something, set it free, and if it comes back then you're meant to fuck it.

Fuck it. Sure, I'm cold. Sure, I'm missing the headliner. Sure, my tent is all the way on the other side of the goddamn festival and I have to cross it, while freezing every inch of my skin off like some cryogenic bullshit. But, I'm an optimist. Gotta find the good in the bad. Look toward the future with open arms instead of crossed ones, closed off to new things and experiences. So afraid of everything that you stay home instead of going out. Metaphorical boy in the plastic bubble. Don't even know how to skateboard. Never learned. Can instead of can't. Will instead of won't. Hell yeah instead of a living hell. It's all so fucking stupid. Turn on the fucking switch. Wake up to the potential in the world. Don't write emails to your boss about how your co-workers all take an hour and fifteen for lunch and anonymously sign them Paulie Carolina. Negative Yelp posts because you haven't had sex since Obama was President. So much easier to pout, right?

But that ain't me baby. Me be happy baby. Make life better. Plus I have cocaine and ketamine. The power couple of powders.

Jay-Z and Beyoncé. Ye-Z and K-yoncé. K-Z and Blowyoncé. This is the best part of the high. When you're not even high anymore. Just high functioning. Seven me's all lined up in a row at the station. Can #4 step forward and say "Give me all your money." May the best me win.

Throwing blows at my negative thoughts like Jackie Chan in every movie he's ever been in. Sure, the fight moves are sloppy, but they're mine and they're defending my honor. You gonna say that to my face? This guy is fucking radical. Kick spin anxiety into next week. And I do mean next week. Blast that shit into the future.

Now it's time to do drugs, and the two bags resting in my hands, waiting to be consumed, beg, saying please sniff me Kevin, and it's like my name's Roland, and they're like we don't care as long as you fucking do us.

And I say okay, but those tricky bags are always trying to get me in trouble. Wind take them away, blowing powders out of nose and into grass, losing money like the stock market dropping on a random Tuesday in September. Minimal trouble over shackles and jail cells. Political prisoners still in jail for pot while Lindsay sells THC massages down at the boardwalk. Trouble ain't worth it anyway you shake it. Lost or loser, nuh uh.

Drug Rule #2 - Don't get in trouble. Police. Authorities. Fuck em. Much easier said than done, but it's the difference between good at drugs and bad at drugs.

HE SAID THE TITLE OF THE BOOK. (again)

The only rule more important than not getting in trouble is

not dying.

Drug Rule #1 - Don't Die. Dying is way worse than going to jail or having to get your daddy to hire you a lawyer. Cause then there's no more life to live. No more experiences to have. No more drugs to consume. I like to think we, as an entire culture, are better than that.

Since wind blowing is a terrible time to do this blow, I duck under somebody's tapestry and into their campsite. I take a seat. It's relaxing. Warm, inviting, friendly vibes. One tapestry has the stars connecting dots into an algorithm of shapes. We've gone over this.

Confident that no one will be coming back for at least another hour, I make myself at home. Crack open a beer and sip gently so as to not freeze further my already frozen throat. The bags itch my palm. Do me, do me. Okay, okay. Fine, you've convinced me.

Flip the spoon out from behind my ear, which is where I would keep it if I were cool. Instead I keep it in the bottom of my pocket, buried deep so I don't lose the only possession I've ever loved. That's not true. I once owned a bike named Randy I was pretty tight with. And outside this fantasy realm—dragons and wizards and psychedelics oh my—I've got a real love/hate relationship with my phone. Yeah, we fuck, but it also sucks.

One to make the pain go away. I'm the Incredible Hulk, and ladies and gentlemen, Hulk smash. Ramped up and ready to go. Party Animal. Animal on the drums. Keith Moon. Who? I ain't cold no more. Ain't never been cold. Could go up to Alaska in just short shorts and I'd survive an entire winter killing bears, crawling inside and eating their meat. I'm a regular Paul Bunyan. The other to even me out, like whatever man, the world's all a charade. The only bears I care about are five smiling ones of varying colors dancing in a line. They've taken a circle, hitching back into the other end and rotating on an axis. Thank Bear himself—Owsley, the man who made acid what it is today (aka what I'm on, keep up)—for going to prison so the rest of us could thrive. Sure, he broke rule #2 but Augustus Stanley was top-tier talent. No ifs ands or sneezes about it.

Woozy. And sure, I could just sit here and relax. Sip at this beer as if it were my own, without a care in the world really. Except that I'm missing the star of the show, the man who convinced me via a steady stream of Instagram posts to buy a ticket, the only artist on the lineup I actually cared to catch. The truth being, and I feel comfortable admitting this now, that even though I was here 5 years ago and I'd listened to dozens of his live sets on the internet, I still have never actually seen him play.

No time for relax. Wake up. Shake out the giggles.

We will cross this festival quickly.
We will change into warmer clothes.
We will make it down to Love Language's set with at least a half an hour to spare.

Thirty minutes out of one hundred and twenty being the appropriate amount to claim I was there. A phrase that James Murphy likes to parse around with a sense of earned snobbery in 2005's "Losing My Edge," a song that single-handedly claims responsibility for "playing Daft Punk to the rock kids," which was a landmark moment in dance music that ultimately changed the entire scene as we know it. If not for Daft

Punk in the Sahara Tent at Coachella 2006, with their LED pyramid production, raves would likely still be relegated to underground warehouses only populated by people with baby pacifiers in their mouths, and not an entire cultural movement valued at over $9 billion a year. Biggups to them French robots.

Power through. Trudge through the snow. What would the stars of hit Fantasy-television show *Snow Realm* do? They'd trudge baby, they'd trudge. So I trudge, skin bare to the frost, powering through until the universe is mine to claim again. It's not even far.

I pass landmark locations that we've covered time and time again, honestly exhaustively. The back of the stage. The stand where coffee is sold and would warm my soul but would also require a stop that my body is not ready for. The palace of eternal solitude.

A bush in the pathway, me stumbling and twisting my body just right so as not to make it face-plant straight into the ground. Face meets plant. Bush in my mouth. Not talking about pussy eating nor former-president cannibalism. Not that I can remember a bush being in the middle of this walkway. Thought I knew my way. Suspicious. Hmm.

The bush pops up from its lowered position to contain a face. A familiar face. One that I've certainly met, but I'm having trouble placing because it's attached to a sort of shrubbery situation that distracts toward context. It's got a real suburban look. Not one I've come to not expect from this mild desert. That's some green foliage for a complete lack of water. Camel humps be gone.

"Hey, man. How'd that acid work out for you?" the bush asks,

156

which places this bush in a very small venn diagram of people I've crossed paths with in the past 24 hours.

That, or I'm hallucinating a face inside a bush. And this bush is in fact just a bush. But that's an irresponsibly incorrect representation of what an LSD trip is really like.

TRUTH: Anything so implausible in a fictionalized trip would likely mean that one had never been off their fucking rocker. Best we get is brighter lights and a swirling sense of existence. Sunglasses of the mind that mess everything up a little bit, but don't leap all the way to seeing elephants with your dad's face on them. The only time one sees visuals like that is in their imagination. Traditionally, while they're staring at the top of their tent, trying to fall asleep. Imagination on fleek, but this isn't augmented reality, pull out a phone and see a Tiger chilling in your living room. It's real life beautified (or weirded up, depending on the dose (or afterdose)).

An accurate description of psychedelics is literally all I'm going for. Sure, I'll take some liberties out for a spin, but I'm not about to meet a talking bush and have him show me the true way. This is for certain a person in a bush costume. Which, in and of itself, is strange, but that's festival culture.

The bush pulls off his hood, leaves and branches nestling on the back of his head, revealing the blue hair I'd recognize anywhere. Not sure if I even mentioned Lexi's blue hair on the first go-around, or maybe didn't even notice it before and am only noticing it now in putting this mental facial reconstruction surgery back together. Don't call it a retcon.

Oh-ho. This guy. Lexi. My friend. The man who put me in this predicament, though not entirely fair to point blame in that direction. I'm the one who put myself in this predicament. Or we can blame my parents for birthing me in the first place. Or their parents' parents. We can trace my family tree all the way back to Christopher Columbus and blame it on that motherfucker (amongst other things) for bringing my lineage over here on one of those dumbass-named boats.

"High. Cold." is all I'm able to stutter out of my throat. Lexi instantly understands, wrapping me in a warm embrace that's as prickly as it is comforting, my body releasing tension for the first time since day turned into night or at the very least since this long (short) journey from campsite to campsite began.

"Clothes." The king of one syllable words that explain exactly who I am and what I need.
"Where you camped?" Lexi asks.
"Up," I respond.

"Okay, let's do this." Lexi spins around me, embracing me from the back, like a bush backpack that warms and follows, a second set of plant-based feet to guide me back to where I need to be.

I walk, and he walks in stride. He blabs on and on about the Brunch set he stayed up until 6AM for, detailing his friendship with a DJ who goes by Lunch. How they went to high school together and even collaborated on a track once back in the day, but doesn't think it'll ever see the light of day because it wasn't very good.

My eyes they are a-rolling, thankful that he doesn't have a view of said eyeballs as I am enjoying the company. He continues on...

"Felt like the Jungle Book kinda sunrise mimosa vibes, even if the sun wasn't ready to show its face yet. That 4AM to 5AM block was so fucking cold I didn't know if I could handle it, so I just went deeper into the dance floor and danced harder to try and get some body heat. Hard to keep up that kind of energy when I already did all my coke. Oh well. Here we are now. Surviving."

I have coke and I want to tell him, but now's not the time. Save my words for after my skin is covered in fabric and not exposed to patches of cold through the errant holes in a bush costume. So instead I just say "left" at the sign of Marshall Applewhite, Mr. Heaven's Gate himself, smiling wide after buying 39 identical pairs of Nikes (discontinued) and a batch of discount purple velvet.

Lexi turns left and lets his ramble out a little longer. Suspect that this man is actually out of cocaine with this kind of motormouth. "That's why I'm in the bush. This body suit is warm as hell." I laugh. Maybe for you.

Finally, with our tents in sight, I release my final syllable for the time being. "Here," and the branch arms release. My body catapults into the tent to cover myself in every piece of warm clothing I own simultaneously.

Bury myself in the sleeping bag, over my head, burrowing in like a worm does to dirt, vibrating away the cold with an exaggerated shivering that reflects the exact amount of energy my body needs to feel warm again.

"Vodka?" Lexi asks from the comfort of our living room, pulling from what I can imagine is one of those pocket-sized bottles, the ones you keep in your back pocket if you need your candy drink on hand at any and all times.

"No thanks, but you can have one of my beers if you want," I answer, muffled through the bottom of a surprisingly smelly sleeping bag, proud for managing more than one syllable, but also that I'm able to communicate loudly enough to receive a "thanks" in response.

The shaking settles and the sleeping bag slowly recedes from my body just enough to get into all the clothing I own. I don't even care how I look. What's the difference? Sweatpants, two sweatshirts, scarves, mittens, a jacket. First day of snow below freezing temperatures. Minnesota, eh?

When I pop my head out of the tent, Lexi laughs. "You look like an arctic explorer." From the depths of the desert to the frozen tundra.

"Too much?" I ask.
"Who gives a shit, I'm dressed like a bush." He shrugs and pulls another swig from the same 375ml bottle (as predicted).

I take Micah's seat because Lexi's in mine, Micah likely off seeing the DJ we'd spent the entire drive up listening to. I delve through layers of clothing to unearth my drugs and toss him the one without the purple sticker.

Cocaine, I tell him, grateful I am able to support him in his time of need as he was in mine. We'll go from cold to lightning hot ASAP. Sweating in these layers and I'll quickly have to remove most of what I just added on.

The K for me. Need it more than any time I've ever claimed to need it before. Bump me back into my body. Even if that body is a mess of limbs, fumbling about, trying to hold on to the edge of the Earth. The cold single-handedly freezing the drugs out of my system on that last go-around. Wasted sniffs.

Shake the bag. More in here than I remember. Thought I'd been dwindling this down to almost nothing, but here it was fully stocked. Fresh shipment. Ready to take on the next day of Black Friday sniffers.

It's in the exact moment that I hear Lexi inhale the drugs that I realize this bag doesn't have a purple smiley face sticker either. FUCK. Purple Ketamine gone out the window, wind-blown away, freezing temperatures melting glue, separating bag from price tag. And here we are, the silent waiting game to what will come of the situation.

<u>What do you think happened?</u>

☐   If you want Lexi to snort the ketamine and go into a massive k-hole, please continue reading as normal.

☐   If you want Roland to be correct and have handed Lexi the bag of cocaine then fuck right off because you've got a complete and total disregard for dramatic tension and it's like how comfortable can you really be in a book where nothing bad happens to anybody? It's your fault things have to happen this way.

☐   If you want to start the book over from the beginning, turn to page 1. It's your life, we're just living in it.

~~5~~

Oh yeah, most definitely the K.

Micah's plan, bound to backfire, did, and expertly. Vomit everywhere. The bush of a man bent over a bush, puking the entirety of his insides out, unable to communicate what was happening to him—not even really sure what that could even be if it were even anything.

Clinical studies have cited bladder issues as the only major negative downside of ketamine use. And that's only over extended periods of time, long term. Which, I'm probably facing, but I also haven't peed in almost three days so take that. Otherwise, if taken in correct dosage, it is a perfect high: controllable, lucid (enough), and sans hangover.

But what they don't tell you on drugreport.net is that ketamine and alcohol don't really mix well. Like at all. Might as well be mortal enemies standing on either side of the plain preparing for battle. The incorrect dosage of one alongside the incorrect dosage of the other is gonna leave you a bit of a barfing mess.

That's why we label our separate bags. So this doesn't happen. I say, as if I had anything to do with that decision and it wasn't my guardian angel Micah looking out for this exact situation as if he were telekinetic too and saw it coming a million miles away. Not everything requires mental powers. Some, just common sense.

Hold back branches, feeling terrible that I ruined this dude's night, apologies to this youth who has been nothing but a goddamn beacon of positive energy. I check my phone—1:11—our time to catch the tail of Love Language's set speedily depleting.

Think think think. Will into existence the kind of solution that doesn't exist for a problem that does. No band-aid for the vomit hole but to ride the wave.

In the mesh cup holder is a bag of powder with a quantity more along the lines of what I expected. Glass half-filled, but that's only because I don't want to admit the alternative. Can't run out of drugs until I'm ready to. Rule #3: Ration. Except not now. Slip over the edge and find common ground, shared gibberish in the jk-hole to laugh our cares away. Spoon in, overfilling the coffee pot instead of the normal two tablespoons. There she goes, and I go with it. Off into another realm. My body accepts the coziness of going all the way in and morphs into a warm blob of—is this what loving yourself looks like?

I lean back and stare up at the stars, the sound of puke in perfect synchronicity with the distant bounce of the DJ, as if a vocal sample perfectly engineered to the beat. Ack ack arrrrww. Ack. GRRRRRhhhfff.

The stars flash and they jumble. Blink and they're in a different place. Like they're not meant to be understood by mere men. Could be: that's why we do psychedelics. To open up and connect to the universe. It's all so small. Insignificant. Glistening, twinkling little bulbs that mean so much more to

163

so many than a couple of computer-rigged lights pointed at a stage ever could. Start the Earth all over again, I don't think anybody would mind.

"Starzs," I say, in a moment of silence between Lexi's dry heaves. To my side, parallel-body, head reversed, feet of the bush in the bush, Lexi lies, awestruck at the galactic phenomenon spinning above his head.

"Starzs," Lexi echoes. Mouth full of marbles, naming constellations with words that will never exist.

Tarvonony. Uckstillin. Linkalver. Caughtinni. Purnesst. Velvelop. Brantif. Carg. Jeep. Blap. Trenviss. Gorgol. Pleana za Vant. Scape du Fromark. Lally. Repeating the phrases the other comes up with as if they are the greatest thing that's ever been said.

"Laugh Language," I add, after a moment of compressed air forcefully pushes from my lungs. A deep breath, sucking in all the stars in the sky and shooting them back out. Inhale, exhale the ground beneath us into stability.

Lexi snorts, the ultimate laugh. "Laugh Language," he repeats. A sigh of relief.

In this moment we defeat our expectations. Throw wants and desires down into the dirt and squish them with the heel of our boots. If we weren't lying on this mat, in the middle of the campground, listening to the set from afar instead of all up in it, we would have never shared in this joke that exists only between two.

What's better than that? A collective experience? 6 billion

people bouncing to the same beat, like the ticking of their hearts is the only thing keeping them going, even though they all have different blood types and couldn't save each other if they even wanted to. This—this is for us.

Reach out to one person, grab their hand and pull them out of the pit. Forge a singular unity where there wasn't one before. We can't make 5000 connections at one precise moment in time. Fingers out and touch the person next to you. Now introduce yourself and say hello. Those connections spread. Six degrees of Kevin Bacon yourself to every other person here, but that's not collective, that's not unity. That's just a masquerade of a shared experience. We're still individuals trapped in our own skin, allowing the dancing and the drugs to be antisocial for us. To pretend for a moment that we're connecting because we're simply around other people.

Sometimes you go to the desert and kick its ass. Other times the desert hands your ass back to you on a silver platter, heart ripped out through your hindquarters and a bit of brain on the side for good measure.

I don't know anything. I've got no idea how to meet people and connect even though they're around me at all times. But now I laugh and language. I love myself. Don't mind that I'm missing the headliner because this is fun too. Isn't that enough? It's never been about the music. It's about the space music creates.

Desperate for a girl or a trip to turn me around. When it turns out all I need is a homie. A good time. A real fucking laugh. There is a lesson here. It's in the unexpected.

I sit up, stars still in my eyes, hearing that same voice from yesterday. Pitch-shifted, calling for me, deep in the trenches of

165

the k-hole, beckoning me to stay. *Stay. Stay. Stay. Stay.*

But it all fades away. The stars in my eyes, the voice in my head. Just me, alone. The bush, disappearing back into the bush. Head down, eyes closed, nothing here but two bushes, man.

"You still with me?" I ask.
Lexi laughs. "Sortof."

"Can you stand?" I ask, turning my body over to the knees and trying to raise myself up.
"Sortof," the bush responds. Exact same intonation, a tape recorder caught on loop.

Leaning on each other, receiving support from a rickety structure about to collapse in on itself, we end up vertical. Back from ground control. Sort of. The planetary depth inside gone from its whirling trip around the mind, the voice still calling out for me. Should we go to the dance floor and play out the rest of the night as intended? Sure. Fine. Sounds great.

"Let's walk."

We come back the way we came. Straight and down the hill still. Round the bend and back again. The music louder, layered, with husky vocals beckoning us to come on down and have a good time, Love Language's hit, "Good Time," mandating our soon-to-be outlook.

> *Have a good time.*
> *Not optional.*
> *Have a good time.*
> *Obligatory.*

Have a good time.
The choice is no longer yours.
Have a good time.
Shut up and dance, willya?

We hit the floor at 1:30 on the dot, our sea legs instantly stable, as if this is how things were always meant to happen. Not there when you want to be, but there enough for it to count.

5

Lexi goes M.I.A. immediately, bounding right in like he knows where his friends are or couldn't care less if he finds them or not. Ah, bouncing back from the brink with the passion of youth. Squirrely climbing a tree looking for me, I lurk around back waiting for something to catch my ear. This is a Love Language set after all. Healing properties.

Can't find the groove. Locked out. Trapped on the outskirts with the other dregs, people with self-image issues, tall, fat, dressed wrong, ugly. Standing in the back because they're not secure enough with themselves to go on in and have actual, legitimate fun.

I try to nudge in further. Immerse myself in those Love Language sounds. Surf's up. Radical. Wipeout. Push past the threshold, by the gatekeepers of cool, and into the hub. Try and connect with the track through full submersion. Lights—check. Music—check. Crippling sense of self-doubt—fuck.

Can't. Unable. Enjoying myself is about as far off the radar as anything in the history of doppler signaling has ever been. Maybe it's me. *Or maybe it's just not that good*, I tell myself like that'll make a lick of difference. Could be he's winding down, setting his brother up for the grand slam weekend-stealing set. Yeah, yeah. Gotta be. Could patch up that nose with a batch of good time potion and maybe I'll be dreaming this music is as good as the people around me seem to think it is.

I start to pace, uncomfortable from skin to scales. At first it's small steps, but then it becomes a much bigger footprint. Neil Armstrong. But instead of faking the moon landing, I'm circumnavigating the entire dance floor. Cut an orange in half. Then in half again. Quarter sphere. Half circle. The inside of a skate ramp.

All the way at the far edge is where I'm able to get the best view of Love Language. The man exudes pure good time rock and roll vibes. His mane of hair bobs along to the beat underneath the three-corner Swarovski-crystal-encrusted captain's cap he's never played without. Hands up, fingers playing along with piano keys he's done little more than press play on. Wish the smile plastered across his face was making me want to try on one of my own.

If this is what I'm here for, but I'm not here for it, then what the hell am I here for? Push myself into it because this is what the social media part of the experience tells me I can't miss. Not interested in desperately shaking my body as a vain attempt of pretending to have fun. It's entirely possible that all these people around me are having the time of their lives, or maybe they're just imagining it. Willing themselves into hype-induced happiness just like Dr. Mongoose teaches.

Gonna take myself out of this equation. See what else there is to experience but the same old that's been happening for eons. Like time never has an end and the beginning is the same as it is now. In the beginning there was House. Yeah, we've heard the rest of the story, Jack.

One desperate last-ditch effort to find one of my few friendships. Might turn the whole night around if you ask me. Take a dip through all the people. The long, slow, arduous journey through the center instead of the easy, lonely stroll around the edge.

I push and I shove and I squeeze and I bump and I say excuse me as I cut directly across the middle into the ever-shifting, up, down, left, right floor of dance, everybody else screaming the language of love, living life to the fullest and loving every second of it, brother.

Here I am, throwing a major wrench in their curveball. So deeply ready to go home to the comfort of a tent, but instead I'm plowing through people, hoping that someone I know reaches out, grabs my shoulder and says "hey Roland, we're right here."

Dreamgirl or drug dealer or dude I drove here with; don't really care. Anyone that wants my presence at all instead of the void that I feel I'm beginning to become. The back of a milk carton. The poster child for someone who should have gotten jealous when all of his friends from high school started getting married and having kids instead of doubling down on a life that isn't proving nearly as worthwhile as it was supposed to be.

Sweat pours down my face. One of these too many layers of warmth, betraying me. Cold on the outside, warm on the inside. A reverse undercooked hot pocket. Step on some poor girl's foot and apologize profusely as she angrily side-eyes me. Nothing I can do. *Sorry. Sorry.*

Pass friends sharing bumps. One bump for you, one bump for

me. Take some of mine, friend. Trade you bag for bag. Two guys in matching wigs switch bags, laughing about it, like it's no big deal to have a positive experience. Casual.

Push out to the other side, reborn. But I don't feel remotely revitalized.

Fuck.

Directly across the way, as if predestined, is the worst possible outcome. Abort this mission for the complete antithesis of a friend. Collapse to the floor and kick my hands and feet into the dirt. Why world, why have you forsaken me? I made it this far, put through the ringer just to face the final boss of the one motherfucker I don't want to deal with.

Ronald. The last person on my whack threshold list. He waves. Come on over.

Caught. His friends mill around him like he's some second coming of Elvis Christ or something. How come they never have anything to say? Mouthpiece for the entire organization. That's how shit like Enron happens.

The most boring questions in the world and he asks them in order:

1. What are you up to?
2. How are you doing?
3. Are you having a good time?

One-two-three-blammo. Blow my brains out while you're at it, holding me hostage with your stupid fucking face and even worse attitude. Got that conversation gun up against my temple. Nobody move or this chump gets it.

I answer with nods and grunts and simple phrases that don't highlight how bad of a time I'm having. Not trying to get sympathy hugs from Ronald. An offer to hang out with him and the mute boys sounds worse than any other possible fate.

I politely decline a bump of Ronald's cocaine, knowing full well that if I wanted to be even further off the deep end than I already am I have my own stash to contend with, but also that taking his drugs would necessitate further communication. AKA: big nah.

Now he's rambling on about Love Language and all the times he's seen him. Four times at Piss Bar before he'd really started blowing up. Twice at Exchange. Sound. Spin. Listing festival credits like he's been to every one and how dare I not have heard of them all. Dropping the names of countries I haven't even heard of. Canadexico. The Republic of Trenjer. I don't even understand how we got here. I'm doing my best impression of a person nodding. It's not so much an impression as a compulsion.

The track transitions and (of course) Ronald has a comment on it. "Oh shit, this is Pierre Dierrere's 'City Girl.' I heard this track when I saw DJ Crumb play in Seattle last weekend. I was up there for my brother's birthday and boom: DJ Crumb is playing?! Tight. Been playing it on repeat ever since. Always turns up." I couldn't give any less of a shit. Ronald makes me fundamentally like music less. Big whoop, making claims like an insurance adjuster.

I'm gonna stop you right there. I use those exact words as I very nearly put a finger to the set of lips that appear to be flapping more than a bird trying to migrate its way to a warmer climate. In my head I deliver this kick-ass monologue about how I don't care and I've never cared and if he just shut the fuck up for once in his stupid fucking life and read the body language of other fucking people in the world he fucking might notice that.

Maybe it's just the finger gently pressed against his lips as if to shush, but he looks absolutely mortified. Or it's entirely possible the words did come out of my mouth. I can't quite control the signal of that brain today—words releasing themselves like atom bombs when I least expect it—speaking truth to self, but also to anyone who'll hear apparently.

I squint real hard and picture a zipper, zipping those lips shut. Sealed away never to be heard from again. High five all of his friends as I hightail my way out of there. Feeling better about my situation. In control for the first time all weekend.

Alone, kicking rocks down a dirt path. This is what I deserve. Hands in sweatshirt pockets, uncomfortable out in the elements while those around me seem ready, willing and able to have an excellent time no matter what comes their way. Maybe I'm the villain. Protagonist and antagonist all rolled up into one like a burrito made of pizza and paella. The one person willing to extend an olive branch gets shooed away— git.

I wander the lonely trail. So many country songs are written about this exact moment. Bumps of powders instead of Miller Lites and a steady 4 on the floor beat instead of strumming the guitar, but the same sense of deep sadness, unable to connect to another person, getting by and by, but struggling my and my. This one goes out to Mary Lou Tucker from

Johnsville, Arkansas. Country boy lost country girl. See ya at the jamboree.

The music fades as I move away from it. Five to ten minutes tops of Love Language's set, but I count it. Easier to say I was there too than try to explain to every single person I come into contact with come morning that I *just wasn't feeling it*. It'll be this whole conversation where I have to justify that I was in a weird place and it wasn't the music's fault. When the real deal holyfield truth is probably closer to somewhere in the middle. The collective was not crushing, likely an indictment of hype even if it's easier to wear rose-colored glasses and call it circumstantial. Fake optimist optometrist.

There's a crossroads at this festival. North South East West, directional universality toward a great time if you just follow the currents and don't worry so much about which direction is which. Sheep. Lemmings. Phish. What am I if not one of those things?

Stand at the edge of the woods and peer through the trees, hoping there's an answer in the dark beyond it being fucking dark. I realize I never even asked this Magic 8-Ball a question.

There's a scowl on my face that's way more committed than I have been to anything in a long time. Sour Cream and Onion chips best describe my current personality. A grumpy bear awoken out of hibernation way too early with not enough food to get through winter.

Standing and turning, doing nothing, but hoping that by standing and turning in circles slowly enough nobody will realize how much of a weirdo I'm being. Once the night was young but now the night is done. A yawn stretches my mouth as if to say, sure you slept already today, but that was medical, baby, and now it's time for the real thing. Maybe emotional and mental exhaustion is just as powerful as the physical.

Take a dip through the food court to consider a coffee—that which feels like my only friend. Maybe the smell of burnt grounds will inspire me to stay awake. Say hello my baby, hello my darling, let's rage with children ten years my junior who can still take ecstasy and not feel the depths of depression for an entire year afterward.

The coffee stand elicits no inspiration, even though the same girl with the same nose ring sits impatiently behind the counter, looking longingly at a stage that she can hear suitably well but has no access to, all because she's decided to make her festival life a business and that's no kind of life at all. At least I get to have fun at the place where people pay to have fun. At least I have that.

Should I just eat this last tab? Stay up all night? Let Dr. Mongoose imagine me out of existence while he plays music and the girl of my dreams stares up at him longingly. What a waste of a trip. No good vibes. No laser vision. No gigantic revelations that bring me closer to connection. Don't think I ought to add any more fuel to this fire.

Check, check. The microphone bounces and buzzes with the flick of a finger. Out of nowhere standing on this once empty food court stage is a puppet. Black mohawk. Green fur. It's not standing. It's behind a podium. Only a couple of inches off the ground. Attached to some guy's hand, I'm sure. Wrist up the asshole turning tricks for bits.

"Hi, and welcome to my TED Talk," a voice gravels at us.

175

Very Henson. Incredibly reassuring. Much the right energy. The puppet takes in its lackluster audience "Doesn't look like people care too much about Teds around here."

He shrugs. "Well, my name is Ted, and this is my TED Talk."

Coffee girl laughs. I do too. Why anyone would be scheduled opposite Love Language is beyond imagination. This fact alone tells me that this is likely unofficial, renegade, special. I edge in closer, taking a seat on the floor directly in front of the smaller, more intimate of stages, cross-legged like I'm seven again and it's story time. Plop me in front of the television.

Ted and I make fast friends. He regales me with jokes and bits and stories of an economic utopia known as Ted land, a puppet performative reimagining of what a TED and/or Talk has the potential to be. I nestle into the pillows surrounding the stage. Don't remember dozing off. But it's welcomed and warm.

MONDAY

Just like any Monday morning on the farm, moon rising up over the horizon and roosters calling cock a doodle do (doo). Dogs running around, waking everybody up for the start of the day. Plate of hot sausage and eggs, maybe pancakes if it's somebody's birthday—which it is, it's always somebody's birthday. Rubbing my eyes, still in pajamas, I'm a wreck until I get my cup of joe.

Pull a sliver of hay off my face, because it turns out—as I'm piecing together—I've spent the remainder of the evening at the workshop stage using a hay bale as a pillow. No big deal. Must've fallen asleep watching the Puppet talk about new model economic systems because I feel about as crusty as the leftover pizza at a child's birthday party. Rub out the hard crystallized little suckers that have taken up residency in the corner of my eyeballs and flick them into the dirt. It's not littering if it came from inside me. Body back to body.

Look around, a voice deep inside my head instructs. A spin— innocuous enough—reveals to me that I'm the only person in the limits of this human's eyeball abilities.

It's the silence that feels important. A complete and utter lack of auditory additions. Truth is I paid good money to have my ear holes filled with sound incessantly non-stop

24-hour-party-people rip a hole into my soul and play me music until I get sick and vomit on the dance floor because deep down our bodies are not hard-wired for this many hours of anything, yet I'm a bit bitter over the current lack of it.

Check my phone for the time. Dead. 0%. Hibernation mode. Take a lap around the food court, peeking into carts and through the back of tents to see if everybody is hiding from me and it's all some kind of practical joke, except completely impractical, totally not worth anybody's time.

Engines off. Generators slumbering. Tents shuttered. Hellooooo is anybody home? No reaction. Yes, we're all here, but in another dimension. You've become a ghost and are trapped in the nether—neither here nor there. This is your land to haunt now. Try your best to frighten us, but with all the drugs and music it's going to be a triple diamond black level ropes course.

I peer into the coffee booth. My old friend. The one whose name never seemed to matter so why would it now? But I look up anyways and read COFFEE PLACE, my voice spilling space where there was nothing, and the name continues not mattering. The challenge of the vague.

Not even any drip-drops of wake-up sauce landing in a new container to start the day. A fresh batch for all the bleary-eyed ravers of the world. Left, wrapped up for the evening—24-hour shifts be damned. At least she finally got her break.

I climb inside. Pick up pots and canteens, but they're all empty. Like the last drop had been doled out on the late-night dance floor and now there were no scraps of sustenance left for me. Dig my spoon into some fresh grounds and whiff it yawl, except it hits like a punch in the face and I have to grab a handful of napkins just to try and blow it out. Finger out the remainder. Pace circles until the pain subsides.

How about real drugs, yes?, if caffeine won't do. In my pocket the bags are mirror twins. Same size, same shape, same color, same same. Hold one in each palm and try to suss out which one is energy. Based on a rough estimation of mass and overall heaviness, I take a shot in the dark with a shot of powder into my face hole, hoping it's correct and I hit the target I'm shooting at.

Buzzer goes ding-a-linging. You nailed it sucker. There's that pep. There's that step. Wake up call for Mr. Becker breakfast is served.

7:52—that's what the red flashing letters in front of my face read—analog time technology is quite uncommon in the year 2099 (jk (? (maybe, (maybe not? (science fiction? (science fact? (one of the above (or all three?) (as Charles T. Asimov states "there's time enough yet for all of us until the clock stops working, and what will happen to time then? What will happen to time then?" (from *Clock Death 2099*, 1977, Schuster & Shannon))))))))).

Way too late in the AM (morning) to be this alone in the world. Not the witching hour(s) anymore. Slept right through TimeCop. More like pre-primetime than sleep-bedtime. On third thought, there's never an appropriate time to be the only one standing at the rave. Somebody ought to be on something at every single somesecond. Uncharacteristic.

That's when I hear the humming. HmmmmmMmmmmmmmm HmmMmmmMmmmm HmmmmmmmMmmmmmmmMmmmm

179

HmmmMmmmmMmmmm, a rhythmic buzzing emerging softly from thou yonder breaks.

60 Minutes reports. Hard-hitting investigative journalism. Hunter S. Thompson and the secret of the ooze LIVE at 9 only on CSPAN. I hop back over the table from whence I came—an exact reversal of the earlier leap, but body facing the opposite direction. In the briefest of moments I feel like a superhero. Oh well. All things fade.

pathpathpath up to **vendorsvendorsvendor**s, but not a single soul emerges with a friendly hello. Solitary me walking this empty husk of a planet, kicking rocks and bushes. Pass by booths full of merchandise for money. Nobody to take my cash out and flapping in the wind.

The humming gets louder, switching from lowercase to all caps. MMMMMH HMMMMMM. MMMHMMMMMMMH. MMMMMMMMMMMMHMMMMMMHMMMM—the pitch and intonation on a steady stream like a river babbling and all of sudden I'm close enough to it to hear it call my name. Come on in Roland. Drown with us! Styx - Come Sail Away. Or was it Come Sail Away - Styx? Whatever, Enya.

Feet in front of feet, eyes on the prize. Until the stage comes into view. And I stop. Physically unable to move forward, discomforted enough by the sight in front of my eyes that they communicate to my brain to communicate to my feet to hold it right there.

Hundreds (if not thousands, yeah definitely thousands) of people sitting, legs-crossed, eyes shut, humming in perfect unison. With Mr. Mongoose Ph-fucking-D on stage orchestrating the hum. Hand up right left down up right left down rise and fall and rise and fall and 1 2 3 4 and 1 2 3 4 and 1. Imaginary baton held on high, Dr. Mongoose brings the hum to some sort of ear-splitting crescendo. The flick of both wrists releases everyone from their near catatonic state. The humming stops on a dime. Everybody but me.

Yet instinct kicks in and I drop to the ground faster than I've moved all weekend. Knees crossed over each other, palms resting on their associated cap. This is blending in. Bugs Bunny asking what's up doc after stepping in line with Elmer Fudd and all his other hunting buddies.

Eyes slowly open, turning to neighbors excited. What did we just experience? Collective shared mind-numbing unity. Yes, me too. Totally a part of this moment and not sleeping during 99.9999% of it. Dr. Mongoose rises to his feet and dusts off the back of his pant leg. He steps to the microphone and says with the confidence of a man that just fucked somebody's wife, "Thanks for trying something a little different with me."

The whole crowd laughs uproariously. Big time FART vibes. "Well how about we get back to the tunes, huh?" Massive applause. Didn't know 8AM knew how to get this hyphy.

The beat kicks back in. People leap to their feet, dancing like they've never danced before. Ecstasy-fueled gyrations, like it had been illegal in this town to dance and a law just passed making it so everyone could dance once again... but if, big if, they didn't dance like their lives depended on it, then they would be put in front of a firing squad for political treason. Real stakes.

"Let's give it up for Fresh Pots!, huh?" Dr. Mongoose adds before stepping off the stage to shake hands and suck face with his adoring fans—dozens swarming him like he's the second coming of the fucking Maharaj-ji or some shit. I look for Noname—Aurora—but don't spot her in the mix.

Fresh Pots! raises one arm to thank Dr. Mongoose for the shout out. He drops it down just as he drops the bass into the mix. The crowd quivers with excitement, albeit dead behind the eyes. A voice repeats the phrase "en-ergy, en-ergy, en-ergy" over the track, pumping people into a mental oblivion.

Everybody on the same tip but me—hum mass meditation hypnosis mind control groupthink whatever you want to call it or at least me thinking the worst after yesterday's showdown with the doctor's 'bad trip' diagnosis—and all I want is to be back in my tent, alone. Unnerved by a bit of good old fascist tendencies spilling onto our paradise. With a snap of his fingers I can see them all lining up to drink the Jerry Juice and head to the mountaintop with their eyes peeled for the spaceship off this planet. I don't like it one bit.

Take two steps back. Slowly. Then another three. Nobody is paying attention to me, but I don't want that to change against my favor either. Somebody spotting me, with their mouth open wide like the end of *Invasion of the Body Snatchers* (as if to say he's not one of us, get him, he didn't meditate, I knew he didn't belong, he's not hip).

Two turns into ten and, just like with any community of change, they're all too self-absorbed to notice the man slowly walking away. How many yoga, meditation, reiki, crystal new-age occult spiritualism meet-ups have people fading into the background without the practitioners even knowing they were there in the first place? Part and parcel.

Not a shot in hell I can deal with this influx of energy, so I'm going to run away and hide until that freakshow of hums can fade out and mix in to something new.

∽

Slam my hand on cold glass windowing. I've never known Hampton to make it out all three nights of the festival, so I figure this is the best bet I have at sharing in this sense of unnerving leftoutedness. Bang bang. The glass shakes in its place, rippling with the energy of impatience. A pause as I listen for any sign of life inside. THUD. Bang again.

"What are you doing?" a voice behind me asks.

I flip, back against the van, pressed to it like I'm paper. Babe stands, waiting for an answer. I mentally see her foot tap and her finger pat the place where a watch would be. The words fumble in my head and it all sounds so stupid so she waits and I wait and we both wait until something worthwhile comes out of my mouth. End up settling on something based enough on truth: "Just wanted to see if you guys were awake."

She eyes me shifty. To be fair, she's probably familiar with this kind of behavior. Some cokehead (she doesn't know from) hollering at their door saying give me more mate, I'm desperate for a re-up. Complete disregard for the clock. Does she know?

I stand panicked, between a woman and her home. Is she going to eat me alive? Dive right through my chest and send my corpse melting to the ground? Reverse me to a memory? She comes closer, extends an arm right past me, and opens the sliding door.

"Hampton's sleeping. Never seen him drink that much. People kept handing him Vodka. And he kept taking it."

She enters; I follow. The air-conditioning on full blast, Babe takes a seat next to her desk lamp. She places reading glasses on her face and returns to her book—*No Mud, No Lotus*—before inviting me to take a seat with a nod of her head and nothing else. Look down the long way of the van to see my buddy sprawled out in the kind of slumber that reads: been here for a while. Drool forming at the edge of his lip, Hampton in full-on starfish.

"You can wake him up if you want. I don't know where he keeps the coke," she adds, before returning to the book, dismissing me completely. I slide past the weed-covered table—a blunt, ready to be rolled, herb laid out in the cone, abandoned— down to where my friend softly snores.

Gently, my hand pushes his shoulder. He bats me away, rolling over on his back. I nudge him again, adding a whisper to the mix. "Hampton. Hampton. It's Roland. Hey Hampton." Nothing.

I look to Babe. She doesn't return my stare. I push his shoulder harder, rocking him with both hands. At one point I swear he gets vertical. Flick him on the forehead. He starts snoring. I consider smothering him to death with the pillow and cutting my losses. Instead, I yell his name. Babe looks more incredulous than angry. She sighs. A big exaggerated one. Can't believe how much you're putting me out Roland, or was it Ronald(?).

185

All you obnoxious white men over 6 feet tall really start to look the same to me.

She charges down the short length of the van and pushes me out of the way. Babe fishes into her purse, pulls out a bag and a spoon, dips said spoon into said bag, and then places said drug-filled spoon directly under said friend's nose. Looks like she went and lied about not knowing where the coke was. Wonder what else she'd lie to me about.

He breathes in, ingesting. A moment—

Before Hampton shoots up in bed repeating the phrase hoo-boy that's a wake up call right there and rubbing his nose like he just left a Vegas nightclub bathroom stall and is now on his way back to the table to blow more lines off some sex worker's ass he just met fifteen minutes prior and was likely going to take back to the hotel room. Do I mind hanging at the slots for a couple of more hours?

"What's up my friend, you here for the re-up?" Hampton asks, calm, cool and collected as if he'd been woken up this way more than once and knew the drill. I look to Babe and she tells me to get the fuck on with it (with her eyes—this woman has an incredible control over the spectrum of anger-associated expressions the face can convey. True master of her work).

Instead: I tell them about my morning. Puppet Ted Talk turned to mass hypnosis event. Words start falling out of my mouth that don't speak well of my mental health, even if they are the actual thoughts being processed by mine mind. Dr. Mongoose has taken control of our brains, convincing people to free-will themselves right out of existence. Blabbering. Beauty Collective with the brain control. We're the only ones who haven't been brainwashed... yet.

Babe holds back laughter, tears welling in her eyes, covering her mouth with one hand to hold in what I can only assume would be something extremely rude and hurtful if said aloud.

Hampton chimes in. "Never heard of the Beauty Collective doing a mass meditation on the main stage before, but they're a weird bunch. Really they can do whatever they want as long as it brings us—" he gestures to the three of us in the van, but also all the others outside— "closer together." He pauses in self-reflection. "I, for one, am sad I missed it."

"Sounds infinitely cooler than listening to you snore all morning," Babe adds.

Yes. Simple enough. Makes all the sense in the world. I'm just in the wrong demographic, that's it. Probably would have been equally disturbed if I saw people rubbing crystals on their nipples or ecstatically dancing without music at all. Summa that real hippie shit. This was just another corner of spirituality making its way into the rave that I couldn't seem to be able to come to terms with.

As if Hampton can visually see the tension leaving my body, he asks, "You good?" I breathe and I nod and I respond in the affirmative. Yeah, I'm good. I'll be fine. Thanks.

"Well, while you're here, we might as well blow some lines." He extends his arms into a sort of freeze frame, with a big friendly smile attached to it.

Hampton climbs out of bed and over to the table. He clears the weed out of the way with his forearm. "Babe, mirror," he asks of Babe in a way that sounds like he's calling her 'babe' and not using her name. Either way, she hands him a large 8-inch-by-8-inch glass mirror. He lays it down on the table, fishes into a corduroy fanny pack and pulls out two MUCH-larger-than-a-gram bags.

Hampton dumps the contents of both bags out onto the mirror. Winter wonderland. He cuts them up with a student id—UC Berkeley class of 2012—into neat individual lines. They look like icicles hanging down from the front porch after a particularly gnarly snowstorm.

He hands a rolled up hundred-dollar bill to me. Wonder if this was one of the ones I gave him. Or was it twenties? Doesn't matter. I lean over the mirror table and take a look at my reflection. Lines of white criss and cross my face. It almost looks like a prison cell of powders. If I were a smarter man I would make some sort of connection to these drugs being a prison, and me being trapped in a cell of my own fate, instead of a passively sarcastic one.

Nose to the edge of the bill and I rip a major whiff, pulling with all my might, trying to hit that sweet spot between drugs not really working and definitely working. Ket hits the back of my sinuses, plucking a harpsichord on an out of tune string, looped around an uvula trying to sing.

Ketamine turns to cocaine. Cocaine turns back to ketamine. Cocaine. Ketamine. Cocaine. Ketamine. Then some more ketamine. And a whole bunch of cocaine. Ketamine. Cocaine. Back to ketamine. Both at the same time. Til our noses are crusted. Covered in dust.

We don't stop there. Babe hands out baby wipes and we

cleanse our drug infested nostrils. Pull up and get high in the process. You've got to clean up to get right. Fix up, look sharp. And we're back at it. K.C. (and the Sunshine Band). A disco ball turning on the roof of the van, the three of us rage and/or vibe depending on the line inhaled that is. Oscillating between vert and horiz as the minutes tick by and the lines lose their count. Rampant flagrantization.

Hampton leans into the front seat and fiddles with the stereo. Apparently, Babe tells me on his behalf, as if he's too humble to divulge, but not to share, he's been producing some original music and is quite proud of a couple of the tunes he's cooked up. Works in Progress.

We dance. They dance harder than I do. Something about familiarity makes it click more. I tell him I like the songs even though they sound like a hundred other songs I've heard before. No new heart, no new soul, no new eccentricities or samples that make them sound noticeably different from all of the other songs in the world. But of course I lie. This is my guy after all. What am I gonna do, break his heart? Not my style. So instead I say "one in a million," and mean it.

Snort and sniff and the blunt eventually gets rolled.

Hampton and Babe smoke, blissed out, strands of smoke swirling around their heads. Babe takes the phone and switches the music. AUX energy transference. Sublime's "What I Got" plucks and twangs into our brains. We sing along, having known every word since as far back as our earliest days experimenting with substances.

We lean and listen as the album plays through, letting the mellow sink us further into the upholstery. Nothing to do

189

nowhere to be nothing to fear just me and my family. We take turns giggling. They pass the joint back and forth. I'm not stoned but I'm feeling good anyways. Maybe this is a contact high. Or the body is just lounging lavish—floating on the sea of carefree.

Whip Hiss. A familiar sound wakes me from my stupor. Hello? Babe hands a whipped cream canister to Hampton. He shoves the nozzle into his mouth. Lean back. Breathe out-breathe in. Go. Hampton pulls the trigger and shoots compressed nitrous into his system. He leans back in a daze, laughing to himself in a slow, open-faced turkey sandwich kind of way.

Babe grabs the canister, unscrews the top and drops the metal balloon inside with a clang. She loads another and screws it on tight—whip, hiss—and hands it to me. The stainless steel of the Nitrous Oxide dispenser chills my palms. About to lay my ass out for the next 45 seconds. Okay, great. Haven't done a whip-it in years. Exactly what I need.

I lean back, ready my lungs—breathing exercises make it all possible—put the nozzle in my mouth and PULL. The compressed gas rushes down my throat, scorching the sides of fragile flesh and yet after a moment it all just feels so NNN-NNNNNNNNNNNNNNNNNNNNNNNNNNNNNNNNN-NnnnnnnnNNNNNNNNNNNNNXNNNNNNNNNNNN-NNNNNNNNNNNNNNNNNNNNNNNNNNNNNNNNNN-nnnNNNNnnnNNN\\\
\\NN
NNNNNNNNNNNNNNNNNNNNNNNN/\/\/\/\/\/\/\/
\/\WWWW-
WWWWWWWWWWWWWWWWWWWWWWWWW-
WWWWWWWWWWWWWWWWWWWWWWWWW-
WW\\

Reality comes back in waves. Concentric circles from outside in. Drops of Hampton and Babe blur in, no sound but the vibratory waves of the gas passing through. Hum.

Babe chortles deep-voiced beats trapped in her own planet nitrous. The whip-it cracker no longer in my hand, but hers. Removed in that blank out like a magic trick. What time is it? I check my phone to reveal it's still, in fact, dead. I ask for the answer that I can't summon for myself.

"10:45," they answer simultaneously, and we all laugh all over again. Hours. In a second. Time flies when you're having drugs. Hampton pulls the trigger and launches himself out of reality. Spaceman gravitational pull moon walk. Babe offers me another—I decline, still reeling from the last one. She shrugs, back to indifference, and blasts herself off instead.

Step out of the van and thank them for their hospitality, but not in those exact words because no one uses 'hospitality' outside of hotel comment cards. They acknowledge me, but are far too wrapped up in the WHIP-HISS-CRACK launching off in Babe's hands to really care if I live or die or even make it ten steps past the van before getting suckerpunched and dragged off to be ritualistically sacrificed to the psychedelic psavior.

5

Back at square one. Psychedelic nose drugs or not, I still have to go face the reality that is unclear, unsure, uncertain and worst of all unknown. Why was everybody meditating? Why did I care so much? Is it possible to separate art from the artist? I take timid steps, watching hawk-eyed to see if anybody is even actually acting any different.

People pass and they mill and they chatter. Some jump and they yell and they shout, mostly minding their own business— not eagle-eyeing back my hawk-eye. No birds of prey meeting in the middle, sharing a darting glance that would send signals off in my head that something is terribly wrong. Owl heads spin.

Things are—as best as I can tell—completely fucking normal.

I stop the timid steps. Not for them to become less timid, but more of a pause, really. Waiting in the way of oncoming traffic to see what's going to happen. Reflective. Might I just be the only one acting weird. Which is even weirder if I really stop to process it.

Man tips his hat and says "how ya doing?" The least I can do is respond.

But I'm starstruck. Uh er but you're the guy—and he knows it too. That cheshire-cat smile as friendly as it is wide offers a nod and a hello, revealing a man attempting, in vain, to blend in, like some anybody despite a legendarily bedazzled hat sitting atop an equally iconic head of hair.

"Love Language."
"Yeah," he extends a hand. "Nicky." I take that hand and shake the shit out of it, somehow surprised even though this is part of the charm of such a small festival—I could name at least 20 people that call him a close personal friend. Though now I can't seem to remember a single one.

He takes the hat off and runs his hand through his hair, releasing the kind of auditory exclamation that signals both excitement and exhaustion. "You up for that mind-meld?"

I nod, not knowing how else to react. He continues on, stealing focus as he's known to do. "Some pretty radical stuff. Way cooler than my set." He laughs. I laugh, trying hard not to agree with my laughter, and also not reveal that no, in fact, I was not there for the mind-meld, and I was, in fact, slightly perturbed by the part I did see, in fact. It lands somewhere in between. So I pick it up with my words, salvaging. Somewhat.

"Got really deep out there."
"Mars, man. Mars. Connecting with the cosmic consciousness? Tapped in. Couldn't think of a more collective act of beauty if I tried. But that's what we're here for, right?" He laughs, letting the hat land back on his head.

"Right."
"To come together as one. Even if just for a moment." He pauses, off in the clouds. I can almost hear him humming to

193

himself. "Sorry, still reeling."

I agree with the reeling part and tell him as much. We share a hug and he calls me a space brother and thanks me for all I do and all I've ever done and all I ever will do. He leaves me with a parting gift that I wish I could receive as earnestly as it's given. "We couldn't do this without you," he says. So genuine. Completely devoid of the sarcastic piece of shit nihilism that courses through my brain at literally all moments.

The smile and the hat and the hair bid me adieu, continuing on their way, two ships passing in the night, a couple of Longfellows. One that matters and one that doesn't. Which was which?

Mind-meld? That's *Star Trek*, right? Don't know enough about that corner of culture to decipher whether that's a good or a bad thing, but Love Language's comforting presence makes me lean toward the positive. Oh well. It is what it is. This is not a pipe.

The faces stop warping. The shouts and screams return to their base place as part of childhood playground memories. Just kids running around, taking things at face value and dancing because they feel like it. Why do I always have to overcomplicate things by overthinking them? Brain shut off. Shut off, brain.

The foot of the hill pauses my stride for me. Largely because hill feet arch at a different angle than traditional flat ground walking feet. The shift in terrain causes a shift in body movin. Not like I'm avoiding running into Micah—who is going to spot my trepidation infinitely quicker than any stranger ever could—or anything.

On that hike climb, passing by tens of tents before: wait, where the fuck am I? This set up doesn't look particularly familiar. Hitting the edge of the trees trying not to go over the edge of our world and into another one. The wooden realm. Take two steps back and circle for a familiar landmark. Head in the clouds or down in the ground, don't know how I got to the edge.

Back down the hill. Camp [??/\??] comes into view. But that ain't right. The wooden sign is only half of the landmarks. This would be like trying to give someone directions around town and telling them to turn left at the Dairy Queen but the Dairy Queen went out of business and is now a froyo shop.

The Heaven's Gate flag is long gone. Musta hitched a ride on the comet. Saying bye in style. Trek up the hill looking for an abandoned flagpole instead of one with a flag on it. Refusing to take mental note of anything but that bald, withered face has really come to bite me in the ass. Nothing to show for my memory exercises but a vague temporal lostness that can only be rivaled by 40 days in the desert. Jesus christ, this sucks.

Dip in anywhere I guess. Here as good as anywhere. Next to a Coleman-brand tent that could easily fit five-to-seven conspirators, sitting inside with hushed whispers, laughing about removing the flag just to spite a stranger. There is a plan where I holler Micah's name and he responds. Micah, Micah! And he goes Roland! Roland! Follow his voice like the car you can't find in a really massive parking garage. Beep beep. Oh, it's up a level. No wait, mid-tiered. There it is, a Subaru Crosstrek. Drive it home and try not to slip on ice and send the whip careening into a storefront.

Stumbling in the dark—except, light—through tents and

canopies with people inside sharing beers, and stories and nose-beers and nose-stories. Always on the outside looking in. Back alley, hiding in the shadows with no home of my own. Garbage cans and squatters, the high-pitched wail of cats having sex. The rain is coming to wash all the grime away.

There's a moment, I feel, where someone is lost in the woods that they think to themselves: *well this is the end. I've really gone and fucked it. There's nothing left for me but to curl up and die, because the odds that I get out of this jungle—you know what? I am going to call it a jungle, (what's the difference between a jungle and the woods after all but animal breeds. No lions and tigers out here, but there might be bears. If I'm eaten alive by bears tonight, this is what I deserve. For coming out here without a compass and a proper set of directions the chances that I survive)—are slim to none. Will take some sort of massive rescue operation.*

I might not actually die, but I'm certainly never going to find my way back to the tent. Not with this attitude. My no-breadcrumb-dropping ass is gonna circle around these same same but different camps until the music winds down and we all hop back in our cars and head back to—

Oh! There it is! There's my campsite. Just on the other side of that girl sleeping in a hammock, straps stretched between the only two trees in the vicinity. Duh. I'd been staring at it for a full five minutes. Micah was there, sitting in his chair, waving at me. "Roland. Over here. Over here, Roland" comes into full auditory clarity.

Teleport over there. A minefield of ways to hurt myself, but I thank the lord that when I got my mutant powers I was #blessed with teleportation. Jumping from one spot to the next with a flash and a bamf (Canada). Comes in really handy if I remember to use it. Always forgetting that I have magical powers.

I stub my toe on a tent stake and come stumbling into our living area, cursing like a sailor and swearing like a child: ouchie, fuck. That really hurt. Turn the pratfall on its ear to pretend like it was on purpose. Slip and slide into the seat acting like cares are for fools and I don't have any.

Pop open the cooler top and shove my hand inside for a can of beer. Mostly ice fishing down to the few, the sacred. I offer it to my friend and he takes it, fuck it why not. Neither of us caring enough about being drunk to feel the need to ration our dwindling precious commodity. SNAP the tab cracks in the can and we sip in silence, each questioning the truth about the other.

Fuck it. I'll speak first. Hip to the hypnosis. Collaborator in the collective. Down with the disease. Clued in by the man the legend himself. "Meditation was pretty mental, huh?"

Without a hitch, Micah stops mid-sip, the can resting on the edge of his lip, trying to suss out if I'm full of shit or full of it. His eyes squint in that way you really only see in old Westerns. If this were a chess game he'd move bishop to B7, introducing himself off the backline ready to fuck up some pawns with a diagonal parlay. He retorts with a question so damning you'd think I fucked his mother. "I was looking, but I didn't see you. When did you show up?"

I sick my Queen on the bishop and flip the script without straying too far from the narrative. I tell him how I ended up backstage (lie) because I'd been chilling with Dr. Mongoose and Noname earlier that afternoon (truth)—I self-swoon

197

at the mention of her name, but pull back when I consider her relationship to the doctor of the truly demented. I've got things to resolve here.

"Should we go back out there? I mean he taught me how to do it after all," I hear myself ask, bold becoming the style of the century. Uhhhh. A big swallow. Gulp. Sure, yeah. I heard the Hmmms and the Mmmms. How hard could it be? Lead a man to cosmic consciousness, NBD.

"Sure." Micah climbs down to the ground and sits crisscross applesauce. One leg over the other.

The best I can get is the flying V, where my feet touch and my legs spread out like—you guessed it—two Vs. He says something, but I'm too focused on trying to determine whether he knows that I'm not a fucking pod person but a real boy, brain on high alert to every eye twitch, lip turn and nostril flare.

"The K?" he drops in the open space I left for internal thought.

"Right, right." I laugh. Of course. Obviously. Into the pocket I go, trying desperately not to bring attention to the fact that I didn't have the faintest what I was doing.

Hand over fist, toss the bag and it lands directly betwixt his legs. Straight to the dome and he's talking like Keanu: woah. He reaches out, offering the bag back to me. Can't see straight enough to get it to the right place. "Tap in. Let's tap in." I don't know what this Matrix motherfucker is talking about, but I'll take the red pill, whatever.

Snoof a fairly sizable sucker. Right up the nostril like I sure know how. Zip her up, pocket the bag, close my eyes and start-a-humming. We're in sync. Acapella group warming up for the big christmas party. Don't want to hit a D-flat when I'm trying to hit an E#. Harmonize, brother. Hit those hums. HmmmMmmmm HmmmmMmmmm.

This feels like a bad idea, but it's bye bye subconscious. Get the fuck out of here man, ketamine o'clock don't got no time for that shit. Nose so stuffed from the last round that I've got to pause the humming just to pull the sinuses apart and really let it hit. Two fingers on each of the nasal passages, ripping air. Don't want any to get caught on the nose hairs. Micah continues humming.

Black. Maybe it's my eyelids being closed and all or maybe it's the nasal breathing between every double set of Mmms and Hmms, but this is meditating. Levitation to the next level. Breach through to the outer realm. The inner realm. Whatever the fucking space between is.

The connective tissue between points of this beautiful collective fizzes and pops, synapses moving from person to person across this fair land. I can sense their presence. Each and every one of them where they stand, telekinesis hitting hard and I can hear halfs and starts of all sorts of conversations. *Can't believe how lucky—You got any extra rolls—My cousin is such a pain in the ass—What do you think of my new skirt? 200!—This is the best party I've ever been to—At first I thought last year's was better, but now I'm starting to think that next year is where it's going to be—Danny with the GHB—Did you see the way she was dressed?—Me and Pat were ripping K in a handicapped porta potty, Carte Blanche were on—Some of these kids have no idea about waste management—spiritually well-endowed—That light sculpture was so rad. I wanna go back and check that out again—*

199

Are you going to Coachella with us this year or what? You have to!
It's honestly so much better than this—Kanye, son of Donda—Did
you see the way she was checking you out man, that's hot right
there?—IloveyouIloveyouIloveyou—The drugs I bought are the
drugs I bought—There's a ballerina in the mosh pit—There's a
bathroom right there. Look!—I just don't really care about house
music—You're my favorite ground score—Anybody bring any
poppers?—We're the coolest we—This parking lot is absolutely
fucked—They definitely oversold this year—Kilometers?—My boss
thinks I'm dead—Pinpricks on a map, all laid out in front of me.
If I could just pull back a little further it could be the county,
the state, the entire united fucking states of america. We're
global. Infinite. Connecting with ravers in London, Berlin,
Goa, Ibiza, everybody having a good time simultaneously
everywhere. I want the voices to stop, but they don't. They
keep rambling nonsense like it matters, overlapping until I
can't hear anything but noise.

The ball of energy between us mixes together orange and
yellow and red, which is funny because Micah has always
claimed his aura was green. Can't claim your own aura color.
That's like claiming your own spirit animal. I'm a Honey
Badger, but that didn't come from me, that came from the
universe dictating it as so numerous times.

How'd we get here? Humming? Oh yeah. I continue—cruise
control—fast transforming everything I've ever known into
one, simple, easy to understand neural network of connections.

Micah's ball of energy turns into a frog sitting on a lily pad.
He ribbits. I look at the mits in front of me, long-ass claws
protruding from little black paws. Fuck yeah I knew I was a
badger. Chest out. Strut my stuff. I got something to prove.
Hello friend.

Shift to the negative. Image emulsion. White is black and black is off-white. I'm not even humming on purpose, but a joining of our voices pipes in through speakers that don't exist. There's no music in here. Just us.

Micah? Swim through space and shout through vibrations a vague approximation of his name. Nothing but another presence. A pat on the back. Something sliding into the spot next to the one I'm theoretically occupying. Like twins in the womb eyes can't open but you know, feel another heartbeat.

Hello Roland, Micah. Welcome to the Everything. 11:11. Synchronicities are not just the question; they are also the answer. Remove your name. Remove your identity. The collective opens its heart to you. Do you feel it beating?

I do. We do. 4,998 (or so) other hearts beat in unison, everyone in perfect sync, lined up and ready, waiting for something, anything to give their lives meaning.

House Music is the answer. Techno is the answer. Unification on the dance floor. One unflappable bond, moving together, thinking together, acting together for all eternity. There's nothing to stop us if we—

"Mushrooms?" A tender voice pushes through, booming in the sphere of our influence. "Mushroom chocolates." Reversal of a time warp, through everything that's ever happened to anyone warp speed tunnel back to reality. Boom, we're in our skin—holding hands—the humming stops.

I shake it loose, but Micah lags—sounds like him—turning my attention to a girl who looks familiar. Coffee? No. *Vica. Vica. Vica.* Vica. Oh shit. The girl from Friday. As my vision corrects itself I remember the memory in crystal clear perception.

Flashback:

As if we'd spoken them into existence, a fairy queen who introduces herself as Vica offers us mushroom chocolates that she made herself. *The chocolate or the mushrooms?*, I don't ask. She tells us the second part before the first, with Micah raising the sleep mask up to his forehead like an incredulous set of eyebrows.

"How much?" I ask instead, more inquisitive than actually interested.
"$10," she responds. "They're about half a gram per."

We look to each other, deciding incommunicado if we'd like to trip on mushrooms or not. Committing to half a gram—or even half a half a gram if we were to split it—of psilocybin on day one was a mistake I'd made before and wasn't about to make again. I remember walking around the forest three miles away from our campground begging raccoons for their mercy. They showed none and I shivered under shrubbery until morning, when by the light of day I was easier to find. Sure I could buy now, imbibe later, but chocolate melts under the hot hot heat and I'm not trying to lick choc off my fingers to make it worth the present me wanting it later. Future me thanks present me for not sucking. Shrooms never come when I want them.

I tell her all of this, and she nods knowingly like gotta make a buck, but I get it buckaroo. She rises from her sales pitch squat, and starts to head off on her way, back to wheeling and dealing, when I tell her to come back later in the weekend and we'll buy a couple, knowing that her returning was about as likely as me still wanting them: an even 50/50. Micah and I wave goodbye to Vica, repeating her name to each other in order to remember it. Vica, Vica, Vica hoping we don't forget it when and if we inevitably want what she's offering. Vica.

Micah comes to, blinking incredulously, completely unable to fathom how we went from there to here in the split of a second. This must've been how that atom felt. $20 emerges from my wallet as if willed into existence, a magic trick that's not so much of a ta-da and more of a money comes and money goes sigh. It turns to her hands and the afore-bargained mushrooms to mine. Two foil-wrapped hearts. Cold. The chocolate chilled from the small neon-pink box cooler she's halfway-to-finished zipping back up.

"Be careful. Maybe eat half." Vica laughs. She rises out of a squat for a second time as if all a memory. "Whatever you want though."

202

The fairy queen skips away, off to brighten someone else's day or at least relieve them of an awkward interaction, while we blink ourselves back from the brink.

"Can you drive back to San Diego?" I ask in a moment of weakness.
"Uh, yeah, sure," Micah responds, weakly.

I find an excuse to be in my tent and not back in the meditation.

∽

Not long after hearing my campmate mumble to himself something along the lines of 'guess I'm going to head down to the dance floor,' I emerge from the tent, redressed and refreshed, a moment to myself making all the difference, with my phone plugged into one of those portable chargers and rising slowly to 21, 22%.

Instantly assaulted by a voice stammering behind me with the intensity of a jackhammer pounding through concrete to make way for Tony Hawk's star on the Hollywood Walk of Fame. "You, you, you, you, you. I know you." I turn around ready to flip a motherfucker over my shoulder if I need to. Fisticuffs up, Bruce Lee Dragon style.

"The war between love and hate has turned tides, man. Turned tides. Don't like what I'm seeing out there." I don't recognize his face, but I definitely remember the four cameras slung around his neck. At least this time he's not harassing me with one of them on the dance floor. His frenzied eyes darting around his face plead for a friend.

"You cool?," he asks. A moment, while I consider a question that's a lot harder to answer than I believe he intended. "Yeah, I'm cool."

"Come, come with me" the cameraman gestures wildly into the sea of tents. And for some unexplainable reason I follow. Up two, cross three, down four, back another row. This is a Rubik's Cube and he must have just solved a side because we're surrounded exclusively by green tents.

He disappears inside one, and I am compelled to go in after.

Flash. His camera up and filling the space between us, the light boring its way down on me. The glare from the viewfinder reflects off his glasses. He moves the lens closer and I swear I can feel the light burning my retinas. Stealing my soul. Blink and turn out of the spotlight.

He lowers the camera, pointing the light into a more neutral space. It lights up his face like spooky campfire tales. The man with a hook clawing at the backseat. At least I can see now.

"You're clear." He seems relieved. "It's the eyes. Like they're not all there," ramping himself back up again into a new, slightly adjacent tizzy. "Do you mind if I film?"
"What?"
"Film. Do you mind if I film? Why would you mind? What do you have to hide?"

"I just—" I try to say, but he stops me before I get much of anything out and raises the camera up. He pulls back to ease the effect of the light on my eyes. I appreciate the gesture.

"This is a real-life *Blair Witch Project*. Don't you get it?" He pauses. "The Meditation," as if a command. "What did you see?"

His fingers twitch and the red light flashing on the black box

205

in his hands tells me the camera is rolling. He moves in. Right on my face. Mouths the word 'action,' enamored with my image repeated 20 frames per second on the screen in front of him.

I tell him what I saw: nothing, really. Just some meditation. The tail end even. Couple of minutes tops. It freaked me out a bit, sure, and I kind of want to go home and climb under the covers and not think about house and techno for a couple of months, but I'm not exactly sure why. Was Dr. Mongoose really anything more than a carnival barker for self-realization?

Our man the documentarian sure seems to think so, nodding along in a way that's almost scarier than the alternative. I need to go, and I tell him that, really wishing I hadn't followed this madman.

"Do you have any drugs?" He stares at me, hopeful. Puppy dog eyes. Please friend, can I have a nibble or a puff or maybe even a sniff. Could turn my whole year around, it could. But my mind wanders back, fragile assurances breaking down, and I can't help but ask—

"What did you see?"
"What did I see!?" he responds, incredulous. "Everything. Got the whole thing on film. Going to turn it into an exposé. What they're *really* doing to your kids at these music festivals."
"Can I watch it?"

He pulls away, protecting the camera, his golden goose. "No, no, no, no. I can't risk it. Then you might buy in too. Brainwashing. Get a little taste and before you know it you're down in Jonestown, drinking the Flavor-Aid because some guy keeps telling you the government has come to take your land away. My Dad was raised in a cult. You ever heard of Righteousness Sons?"

"No."

Inspiration strikes and he cycles through his footage, laughing to himself. He snorts and chortles, howls and giggles, completely forgetting there's another person in his presence. I'm doubtful how well this guy functions on the day to day. I should go.

And yet, I say, "If you show people the footage of the brainwashing, won't they get brainwashed too?" Do I even believe this?

He drops the camera down into his lap. The shadows play on his face and make it appear 10x more somber than it possibly could in real life. Real stark contrast. Pouty lips almost like clown makeup wrapped around the upside-down smile.

THWICK. A quick piece of plastic drops out of the camera and into place. A small black memory card, no bigger than a thumbnail, rests in his hand. He places it as far back on his tongue as he can and dry swallows the memory.

"You're a true hero," he says, saluting me, in what I think might be somehow the least ironic action I've seen all weekend. His head hangs in despair.

"I've got mushrooms."

His eyes light up. Gone is the sadness of his own personal *Gimme Shelter* down the drain. Altamont into not all-that-much. I reach into my pocket and hand him the two haphazardly wrapped chocolates.

There is not a single moment of hesitation. Like a frog's tongue shooting to capture a fly, he's got those suckers unwrapped and down his gullet in a flash, chasing that card full of memories with a whole batch of new ones to come. Thank you, thank you. He repeats himself. Thank you, thank you. If Terence McKenna is to be believed, and mushrooms are spores from alien planets, then perhaps that's where this guy is from too. He smiles wide, chocolate stuck in the reservoirs between his teeth.

"Oh, I got something for you."

He flips the camera over, shooting the light down into his messenger bag. Items scurry about under the duress of searching. He quite nearly sticks his head inside, burying his entire upper torso in the bag. When he comes up it is with heavy breath like almost drowning in a puddle of his own sick.

A vial. He holds it in the palm of one hand and positions the camera above so that the light shines down. The ship back to his home planet picking up a hitchhiker on the side of the road with this tractor beam of a flash.

"It's empty. But there's a wash in there for sure. I'd rinse it out for myself, but I took a ten-strip last night and I need to change psychedelics to get my rocks off again. You do L, right?"

I thank him and take the vial. Bury it deep in the pocket. This was the come up I needed to make my day right. Trading one heady-ass mind trip for one I know clear as day. We share a bump of blow—not that I think this dude needs more energy. It seems boundless.

It shoots up his nose and the speed with which he rambles about lost footage and the only people who know the truth doesn't change in the least. I can't decide if it's reassuring to not be alone in this sense of conspiracy, or worse that I'm sharing this very isolating purview with—him.

When he starts in with the deep rumbling giggles, I know he's gone. Everything I say is the funniest thing in the world. I like to think I'm interesting, but don't know about particularly laugh out loud hilarious. Tried an open mic once and bombed so hard I cried myself to sleep for a week. That's not entirely true, but my girl at the time tried to make up for it with some sympathy sex that I couldn't get hard for. That one two punch really set me on an existential crisis that is probably what led to the end of our relationship. Now that I'm putting all those pieces together, it is fucking hilarious.

His head leans back, rolling on a tilt, eyes closed, moaning uhhhs and ahhhs and whuus that exist somewhere between orgasm and fireworks. I grab him by the shoulders and his eyes open wide, pulled out of his dream-like fugue state and into the reality that he's in his tent with a stranger.

We share a parting moment. As if this were goodbye forever. A bonding experience where I least expect it. High five like we've been practicing for years. Hollow-cup sound of flesh clacking together, fingers wrapped perfectly around palms.

Winding my way back toward civilization, with a brief respite at the abandoned camp [??/\??] where I spot a full water bottle sitting on top of a plastic table. Seemingly abandoned. Store bought, brand name (pick whichever one the heart desires), and yet it's reprehensible to have brought plastic in the first place. Reusable only. Reduce the carbon footprint. Leave no trace. I decide to punish this anonymous donor by donating the bottle to myself. Test the crack and hear that fresh snap. Keep on moving so I don't be been caught stealing.

This is a judgment-free zone. What I do with my drugs is up to me. Micah is definitely on drive duty now whether he wants to or not. Sorry buddy. If the mind wants to be wrong— begging me to be all kinds of fucked up—well then, I fear I must comply. To beeee on marsssss maybe then none of this would seem so weird.

Squat down next to a tree. Right out in the middle of the open. Peer over my shoulder even though I know nobody is looking. I've got to be the last thing on the minds of these empty husks of brain cells making way for the end. Parasitic depths that can only be dreamed by those who've never dreamt before. Do my best to avoid being too obvious anyways. Twist the blotter top off the vial and bite down with the edge of the top. Peer inside. It's empty save for a drip or a drop, glimmering a translucent rainbow.

Twist the cap off the bottle and gently gently gently pour a modicum of Hydrogen (and half that amount of Oxygen) in. Chemicals baby. Hoh! Fill this empty-glass tube just about halfway. Place it down in the grass. Gently resting there, chilling. Like a baby swaddled in cloth. Jesus Christ body and soul. Twist the cap back on.

Shake it up baby now. Shake it up baby. Twist and shout. They say that the proper mixing time is 2 minutes and 35 seconds for all particles to dilute properly. This is a fact and not some gobbledygook I just cooked up. I don't make things up for my own benefit. That's absurd and I won't stand for it.

The half-filled vial has certainly got its rainbow on. Like a puddle after a rainstorm instantly switching over to a beautiful day. How'd it get so nice out; it just rain?

Two ways to consume. First, I could squeeze a couple of drops onto my tongue and hope that takes. Pray that enough of the remaining particles of Albert Hoffman's lysergic-acid derivative have made their way into these specific drops. Or I could just drink the whole wash. This is not advised. But it's what I do.

It goes down easy, like water is supposed to. The smooth ride of scentless chemicals. What did I just take? Who knows? Acid wash is always unpredictable. This rocket ship is no longer in control. Somebody cut the brakes and we're careening off into space, but at least now we're going out the way we want to. Sunglasses on. Pop out of the squat. This is sparkle motion.

5

The dance floor is truly a sight to behold. Acid's coming on woozy in the way, stomach flipping butterflies. Sights for sore eyes transforming out of the cocoon and into something beautiful. I'm overcome with everything. Sun shining down, filling the warmth of my soul. Gorgeous dancers with white teeth protruding between parted lips. Heads bobbing, shoulders bent, bodies in motion, swirling and jumping and immersing.

Let it all go. Stand still and stare up at the clouds. Thick and white and hung in the sky. Not the bleak grey of a storm on the horizon, but clear as day. Clear minded and full of opportunity.

Float on. High above the grounds, birds-eye view of the brainwashed, not minding so much at the prospect. Complacency in mind control. Better here than there. We could never leave. These hundred, turning to hundreds of thousands, and before I know it I'm eighty. Been spending the last fifty years of my life in direct connection with the souls of others. Inside something that mattered. Riding high on a high. Not high to escape, but to be in. A spirituality in connection. People of the sun.

The music spins out. Struck into a single beat, isolated, running up speed until it's batting right up against itself. A frenzy and then silence. I'm pulled back to Earth. Off the cloud and to my feet. Eyes pull down from the sky to the stage. Those around me stop moving and settle into some post-movement stasis that one could, at most, call a sway.

Trevor stands at the decks, an empty booth behind him cleared just for the occasion. He looks like a guy I'd hate in reality, as if he'd spent a former life in finance but recently discovered the benefits of having a good time and practicing self-care. Yet somehow simultaneously humble. A true conundrum dug from the salt of the earth. But what do I know? Never met the guy. He's so soft spoken that we all have to lean in just to make it out when he mumbles, "I know y'all have places to be, but thanks so much for sticking it out with us til the end."

The end? Yikes.

"Yeah Trevor!" Someone screams from behind me. He turns away, bashful, before re-centering. Never one to bask in the spotlight even though the spotlight always had a way of finding him.

"Just gonna warm up a bit for my brothers. Shut up and play the hits, right?"

Track starts up slow. Dripping drums, slathered on the snare with a little bit of an extra rinse to them. On the one-beat, a single piano stab. Dunh—3 more full measures—Dunh. Vocals come next. Indie darling belts out cleverly patronizing lyrics about wanting a hit. But maybe they don't do hits? A pause in the music—before a big, grinding electro bass comes blasting out of the speakers. The entire dance floor explodes with energy.

Fuck. This is what it's all about. Fumble with the zipper to unclasp the bag. A middling amount remains. Turn it onto the corner so it all collects and I can eyeball what's left. Will make it through even though I have to take increasingly larger bumps with each outing just to get where I want to be. After my self-dug k-hole I'd probably really have to go for broke. Dig in without a particular care for quantity, shoving the whole thing up my nose who cares even.

That's the vibe. Music breaks into something else, Trevor riding the mixer quicker than most, selecting a request for mood change-up and refusing to let anything play out longer than a minute or two. But it's this manic energy behind the decks that takes focus off the man twisting knobs. The floor is pumping like we're up there selecting them ourselves. So excited to play the next track that we jump ship, up and around, constantly layering the drums so as to do the job we were brought in to do.

Find myself drawn further toward the stage. Gravity's pull and I can't help but give in. The sea of people parts for me. Though not in a straight line. Left at the dude in the photorealistic zebra mask. Climb under two girls on their boyfriends' shoulders practicing the sacred dance of patty cake. Right at the Squirrel talking with the Bush. Give them a nod. Can't stop and say hello. Their pupils swirl around their sockets, teeth-clenched and heads reared back, laughing. I don't even know if they see me.

Close my eyes and hum along to the beat. If not in rhythm because my vocal cords can't move that fast, then at least in tone with the music puncturing the air around us. Put myself in their shoes. I can see the vibrato of my voice, fluctuating waveforms green and yellow for high and low levels. Don't redline. Everything goes black again.

Levitating in the void. Presences pop up all around me. Left and right and front and center fizzing colors form the shapes I've come to associate with people. Second sight. Seeing with my eyes closed. Really seeing inside the people on the dance floor. The good they've done. Their hearts pumping with compassion. The joy in their ears. And they can see me too.

I feel like one blood cell floating down stream. It takes all of us working together to make this body work, but we're doing it. A living, breathing, walking, talking unanimity. What's the point of being alone when together can feel so warm? Fought it long enough.

The bush and squirrel catch up, standing directly in front of me when my eyes open. Though I already knew this is what would happen. Prediction more than predilection.

"Hey!," we three share in excitement.
"I thought that was you," Lexi yells over the music, the speaker so close we can reach out and touch it. Squirrel leans in and asks what I thought of the L. I answer honestly and without reserve that it was weird. I can tell he feels a bit dejected, but it's true. It was weird. I'm glad to see him and tell him as much to ease the mood a bit.

Lexi yells again. "Thanks for taking care of me last night. Sorry I lost you after."
Squirrel grabs me by the shoulder. "Do you have any K I could buy off you?"

I think for a second about Hampton and how to get him from here to there, but it all seems so complicated and I'm high and

215

I'm having fun for a 'first time, long time' and don't feel like taking on that responsibility. Selfishly, I say no, but tell him I can bump him out if he wants.

He thanks me profusely, tells me that would be awesome, which doesn't sound particularly squirrelly to me, but whatever, we can't always live up to our names or our highest aspirations. Shoot for the stars and you'll land somewhere in between.

I reach into my pocket and pull out the bag with less in it. "You want some blow too?" I ask because I don't even want it anymore. I only bought because it's a capitalistic system and we're supposed to buy things, right? Supply and demand. Me want some, and thus me must buy enough to make sure me have what me want at any and all times. It's not an ideal workaround but I guess that's the price to be paid. Money in, money out. We should all share what we have. The baker bakes bread etc...

Small, Medium or Large? He takes the medium. Reasonable. I fill my very deep spoon about a third of the way up and bring it to his nostril.

Squirrel's wet little nose twitches and pulls. The packed together particles shoot right up into his brain or bloodstream or however nasal passages work. No conflict. Unlike mine getting caught up on well-worn tubes of gunk, powdered boogers and hair. Smaller passageway to push through. Indiana Jones fetching his hat from underneath the wall. Stand clear of the closing doors please.

Offer one to Lexi, but he laughs and shakes his head no. I like this kid. Learns from his lessons. Take his for myself. Hit the other nostril with a batch only a few specks smaller than Squirrel's. Double dipping. But at this point my nose is so fried it's like does it even work or am I just feeding the placebo demon? Clasp it shut and trade it out for the blow.

Fat bump to Squirrel. Fat bump to me. Fat bump to Lexi, peeling back his leaves to get a taste of the coca. I'm here. I'm spinning. I'm in it. I'm giving people bumps on the one beat. We bumping. Trying to off load this bag. Don't want nothing to do with it. Nothing good can ever come of leftover gasolina.

Strangers forming a polite line. *I'll take one. Yeah, me too.* Cousins coming out of the woodwork after you hit it big on the lottery. Cute girl in a Leopard Print leotard. *Thank you very much.* Dude in a Crocodile Dundee hat, outback flipped up to one side. *Alrighty mate, crikey that's some good yayo.* Three girls in green wigs. *Yes. You're the best. I needed that, you're seriously a life saver.*

Oh wait, make that four. The fourth girl has her own spoon on a chain around her neck. She dips hers into my bag, as if she's afraid to share germs with a stranger. Imagine being terrified of snot and trying to rail drugs through your nose. She asks if she can give one to her boyfriend and as I nod yes the bag is gone, back turned. I don't care. Come what can, come what may.

Turn my attention to the DJ. Purists shame the new generation of ravers for giving too much focus to the DJ. They're all facing the same direction, they complain. Wah, Who cares? Why does anyone care what anybody else does? My whole body tingles and I can barely feel my extremities, brain trying desperately to shoot through the top of my head. I feel like a million bucks and that's thanks to three people: the man playing music, the man who gave me more acid than I clearly

217

knew what to do with, and myself.

I guess there are more people involved. Like the man who crystallized this batch—an unknown soldier in the war on the war on drugs. Albert Hoffman for discovering it in the first place. Leary and Alpert and Kesey for popularizing. Whoever actually made the song that's currently being played. The pioneers: Frankie Knuckles, DJ Pierre, The Belleville Three, Giorgio, Kraftwerk. The Beauty Collective. Everyone who helped put this thing together. Everyone here. All coming together into one great big perfect moment.

Life itself.

I can sense Aurora's aura before I can actually see her. Purple pushing through. Two people over three back. No hesitation. Abandon the company of flora and fauna by my side and make my way straight to hers.

The fourth Girl in a Green Wig has her spoon lifted up Aurora's nose. She pulls back embarrassed, red-faced, caught in the act, sharing my coke with everyone in arm's reach like I'm some coke chump and not a coke charity. She extends her arms out to me, making excuses that she was just about to bring it back.

"Keep it," I say, pushing her away with indifference. Don't even take the time to register the look on her face as she recedes into the crowd and I'm pulled in by a purple tractor beam.

Aurora is as frozen as I am. As if time itself has stopped only for us. The rest of the world continues on in fast motion, sped-up dancing looks like a cartoon. Or at least a cleverly edited YouTube video. Music drowns out. We stand still as the second. This moment can last forever if we let it. Trap it in a bottle and keep it on a shelf, high and out of reach, so we can take it down and sip from it anytime we need to remember.

It's all gone. Ripped back to reality. Music in motion and speed set straight. The back of a purple paisley glitter-encrusted suit jacket splits my vision from hers, pushing me back into the crowd of dancers doing what they do best, dancing.

I remember why I'm mad before I completely understand it. The tip of Dr. Mongoose's chin turns to me first. Grey goatee whiskers implanting some rage-inspired hate mail. Dear Dr. Mongoose, I hate you with all my heart and soul. Eat dirt and die a slow and painful death. Sincerely. He turns to me, shit-eating smirk riding up one ear like it's his god-given right to do me wrong. The crowd closes between us.

Sit down. Right here in the middle of everything. This must be what it feels like when a tornado comes through town and the only option is to hide under the table. A whirlwind above and I'm huddled into a ball hoping it all doesn't come crashing down. Close my eyes and wish with all my might for Dr. Mongoose to have never even existed. My only option is to use his own ideas against him. Imagine him right out of here.

He pops like a thought balloon, separating into a thousand pieces and spreading across the globe. A fine mist of never has been erasing its memories as he goes. No longer a recollection of interaction, just another face amongst the thousands. No effect on me but that I let it. And I refuse to let it. Self-doubt sneaks in, as it's known to do. How can I just imagine imagining? Without context. This isn't my idea. It's somebody else's. Hmmm.

Fuck this. Eyes open. Step up. Get to my feet. Charge right over and put myself right in his face. Big tough guy. Barrel-chested bravado. Say something trite and hackneyed like *what's you're fucking deal?* Real high school fight energy. I'd be down to throw a punch, but not here. Maybe at the steering wheel on the way home.

Mongoose squares up. Stops dancing, sets his shoulders back and locks his eyes in combination code with mine. The faux concern on his face reads 'whatever could you possibly mean?' but his body language is a novel entitled *Come At Me Bro*. It's a self-help book with the subtitle: *A Quick and Dirty Way to Realizing Your King of You're Own Mountain* (his typos, not mine). Sold really well through Instagram ads, but never really made the big push to Barnes & Noble or B. Daltons. The sect who ate it up were also the ones who fell hook line and sinker for Bitcoin right before it burst.

"Yes?," he asks like I'm the biggest bother in the universe. At odds through time and space. A real throp in his side. But I don't have much of an answer. What did this guy even really do to me? Edge me out on a girl that isn't even mine? Remind me of the self-value I already carry with me everyday? Show me what I mean to other people? Fuck. Where is she? Nowhere in sight as if she was never even there in the first place.

I want to pull back. To run away. To pretend like none of this ever happened and I'm not making a fool of myself. But it's too late. The circle around us widens. Murmurs from those close enough to see what's happening that I'm some kind of asshole. An army of the same face backs him, and I'm alone. So very alone. Like that one guy who was on a creek once and he didn't have a way to make his raft go.

A point of no return. Backed all the way to the edge of the cliff. The only way out is through. Take the leap. I tell him exactly what's on my mind in the most precise and cutting way I know how.

"You've got seriously bad vibes."

Those around him are shocked. Hands on foreheads. Narrowing of eyes, furrowing of brows. One woman switches into fight stance, mimicking the bobbing motion of an idled Chun-Li straight out of the Street Fighter II arcade cabinet. Waiting for an opponent, up and down, ready to go, tell me when to pounce boss man.

Trevor mixes in the "Cha-Cha Slide" and I can't tell if it's ironic or iconic. Either way it deflates the tension. Clapping hands, moving left, taking it back now, hopping, stomping. Cha-cha-ing real smooth like. Makes this display of masculinity too silly to sustain.

Laugh out loud in a way that none of us can really wrap our head around. Like an inside joke between every person that's ever wanted to find something funny. Rolling on the floor laughing my fucking ass off, but instead we're following the directions of the song. Do as we're told no more, no less. Now it's time to get funky. We hop, step, slide and crisscross like this is some music-video shoot and if we can't cut it we'll be shipped off to Vietnam to fight a war nobody could seem to wrap their heads around either. I lose track of Dr. Badvibes.

Must have shaken something loose inside. Acid powers active because I'm flying. Class A Fighter Jet dive bombing between the clouds. Pushing the limit to the edge of the stratosphere and taking a nosedive into the Bermuda Triangle. Just for fun.

Out of nowhere like a switch my whole body tingles like stardust desperately trying to shoot out of my pores. That moment where a water balloon is about to burst, but not quite, hanging on the edge of together and splattering some middle schooler in the face. Like metaphors are mealworms and all the comparisons are trying to make a life in my corpse.

The people around me fade into the distance. Can't see much of anything. Not that I even want to. Who are these people to me? When I'm me. The best me I wanna be. A fully realized holographic performance art piece. Five Star write up in the Woodstock Gazette. "This guy's the real deal." Frying.

I'm buzzing. Following the steps back and then the steps even farther back. I nearly fall full on my ass, but I'm saved by a kindly gentleman in a three-piece suit. This is the funniest single thing I could possibly see. Which, in this condition my condition is in, tracks.

He lifts me back up to my feet, but I'm so bowled over with laughter that I drop to my knees anyways, slamming my fist into the dirt. A suit! Primal, really. Living out the best-case scenario of what I guess was evolutionary reality. I don't feel particularly evolved. This dude's face blurs into something I don't like so much so I make a run for it. FBI. Stock Trader. Not about to find out. Pushing through and carving out a path to freedom. What was I running from again?

5

Enough hops back and I find my own little patch of grass. It's in the middle of a walkway, sure. But to me, it feels like Paradise. People can walk around if they need to. It's a s-o-c-i-e-t-y after all. Instant calm. A cold shower on the hottest day of the year, finally having sex after an embarrassing dry spell, sitting on the grass listening to music.

I melt. Into the grass. Spread out into a puddle as wide as rain. It's possible that I took too much. But then again, it's also possible that I took just the right amount. I wonder how my man with the mushrooms is feeling. Probably asleep in his car, or maybe out wandering in the woods until he stumbles on a witch's house and gets baked into brownies.

Trevor's music bounds off the stage with undeniable ENERGY shooting directly into my soul. As if it's a concoction of healing properties meant for this exact situation. Get better buddy, everything's gonna be just fine. We're all in this together. Hard times and good times are all the same. Part of the experience. Could've fooled me though.

Sit up. Lucid enough. Until some girl in a tutu nearly trips over me, and her man in a neon sleeveless shirt that says NEON GENESIS gets aggressive in my general direction. "Can't just sit in the middle of the road, buddy." It's like yeah, for sure, but also, what else am I supposed to do? Stop to be? Plus they don't even look cool. Look like they just walked out of a photoshoot for Basic Raver Monthly Catalogue.

Apologize anyways and scurry out of their way, digging up dirt as I pull myself vertical. I turn, with a smile on my face, and I don't stop turning. Not for no one, no how, not even for me. This is my stasis—turning slightly with a grin from ear to ear. Zen in the moments of overstimulation. As both the Doobie Brothers and the Grateful Dead—my father, a fan of both in equal weight—said, "listen to the music." That's what I'm doing. It's all I can do. Lazy Susan and listening in. My brain absolutely melting out of my ears. Ffwonk.

Shot in from the deep trenches of outer space, telepathic, or maybe bouncing off satellites, but it comes like only the best of ideas can: in a flash, rim shot off the metal plate, down the spine and straight out the ears. I must go to Aurora's camp.

Snicker and tiptoe my way through the crowded compartments of people, feeling like the bad guy in a children's movie. My head on swivel, bringing one finger up to my mouth and telling anyone who looks my way to shush, shhhhhh… being very sneaky.

I know the way. All too well. Enraptured enough upon the first go around to pay the utmost attention. Over the hill and through the woods. Up the valley. Cross the river. Follow the train tracks. No wait, that ain't right. Backtrack a couple of hundred feet until I push through to a sight for sore eyes. Prairie Home Companion except I'm the one boring you.

Back flush against Aurora's airstream trailer. Her scent wafts through a cracked window. A mixture of moss tennis courts and lavender fields. A scent I'm only piecing together in retrospect. Maybe a little bit of sage to warn off bad energy—which clearly wasn't doing its job if she spent this much time around Johnny Macaroni aka Dickwad Jones aka Dr. Richard 'Larry' Mongoose.

Peer my head around the corner in the least (most) obvious way possible to see if there are stragglers in the common area. Doesn't look like it, but I try out my bird calls just to make sure. Real peacock energy. The male peacock makes an insufferable noise like NYHHH NYHH and I only know how to mimic it because of the hours of practicing I've done in front of the mirror. Peacock feathers are like turquoise rings or faux leopard print to these hippies.

"Hello?" she responds, opening the door and taking two creaky steps down her front walkway. I emerge from around the corner and the look on Aurora's face registers as disappointment.

"I, uh—" have nothing to say. What was I looking for exactly? Symbiotic relationship of need and known. Who am I to her? Some dude she shared a moment with once? Bleak. Cautionary tale if I've ever heard one. My head is swimming and I can't find the words to help fix this moment. I reach out because words don't come. She scurries back.

I see everything. Where I went wrong and where I'll continue to make mistakes for the rest of my life. She doesn't even need to say anything. There's a whole society out there begging for me to return to normalcy. Back to basics. Take my dog for a walk. Call my Mom. Quit doing drugs. Find new friends. Give up on music altogether. Buy into the system. But that's not the case for her. This is her home. This is her everything. *Cha-Cha real smooth.*

225

"This is all kind of weird." Aurora shuffles her feet just as every other girl who ended things with me has. "It was nice at first, you and I... but I'm gonna go, okay?" she says gesturing with her thumb to anywhere but here.

"But—," I say, as every 'let's see other people' conversation must contain.

She locks up the door to her home without lifting her eyes from her floor, likely taking the moment to concoct some extra excuse beyond. Now that I've made it necessary.

"Look," she says. It's not you it's me, I just don't feel that way about you, You're getting rather clingy, the sexual chemistry is gone, I don't find you physically attractive, I think you're cool and all but not the kind of man I can see myself raising kids with, maybe next year, get a job, I'm more into alpha men to be completely honest, you have a small dick and a big gut and a receding hairline, we come from different worlds what am I supposed to do leave my life behind and start anew with you, it was just a fling and it doesn't have to be more than that, why are boys always so fucking clueless, your friends don't like me, my heart has been removed and replaced with a valve I am unable to feel human emotions like this love you seek, we're just better apart, the spaceship is coming and you're not on the guestlist, I sometimes fuck Dr. Mongoose and while I am technically allowed to see other people it's definitely not encouraged, you're barking up the wrong tree pal I'm a tree, you're really pushing things further than I feel comfortable with yes we kissed and we rubbed backs but it's not like you're not the first guy I've done that with. "It's not real Roland. I'm a flirt. Sorry."

I'm gutted. Heat flashing on my cheeks, survival instinct kicks in and all I want to do is run. I try to say *but* again just to keep her here for one second longer, but she's off, moving past me, stopping only for a moment to pat me on the shoulder. Like a pal.

Bye forever camp bae. That did not go as planned. Kick anything, but mostly myself.

Now what? Fuck.

This is what both my brain and my stomach say simultaneously. While my heart is hurt and my brain is broken the sudden rumbling in my stomach has taken full and instantaneous priority. GrrRibbitSlosh. Empty and full at the same time. Oh, an emergency? And here I am with no fucking clue where the bathrooms are. Comeuppance.

RVs have bathrooms, right? There's an RV right across the way that might do the trick in these desperate times. It's painted to look exactly like the Further bus with the dayglo dreams of one group acid session gone quite crafty. I simultaneously hate it with all my heart and love it with every fiber of my being. Real duality inside me. Is this the best festival I've ever been to or the worst?

No time to answer, barely holding myself together, dodging under tapestries and between lounge chairs. Please be open, please be open. The handle opens on the first try and I thank god, even though we haven't spoken in a while. Three steps up, eyes on the prize that is the back door. Rip that shit open and for lack of a classier way to say it, shit...

What better reason than the bed looks comfortable and I'm physically and emotionally exhausted to take it for a test drive.

Lie back and stare up at the ceiling. All this time I'd been thinking one or two doses was cutting it, but the more that I'm on now is—well—better. The ceiling moves, the lenses of my eyes twirling a merry-go-round of shapes intertwining. Colors in and colors out, colors taking over the show and switching entirely.

The world won't stop spinning, but that's the point, right? I'm just a tiny insignificant dot on an even larger insignificant dot, hurtling through space. I see it all laid out before me on the roof of this stranger's home. I'm a small nothing. Cosmic Joke. Disconnect the dots and reassemble them back together in one. It's not so terrible being alone.

There's a whole visual codex here. This thin outline of a hallucination where I can pull from reference files on anyone in the world. Open a drawer and let the information pour out in a rainbow animatic. Sit up, and it all fades away, a colorful shadow behind a separate complementary color's shadow, a world wide web of everything.

Rip some K to really see this through to its logical conclusion, high on only one supply instead of all of all of it. Lie back and swim, lost in the ether, removed from this here planet into the realm of gods and goddesses. Self-actualization is a hell of a drug.

We meet, she and I. The voice that had been reaching out. A warning or a welcome invitation or maybe even both really. A warmth. An embrace into the fold of all there is and can be. There's no use for words, because it's clear for the first time we're on the same page. Accepting my limitations. Can't go any further alone. *The 12th realm of the 3rd sector. 62nd Projection, 5th wave.* Me. Them. Us. I get it now.

228

The door opens and I shoot up in a cold sweat. The foreground disappearing in the blink of an eye, settling back into the reality that I've taken over some stranger's RV. Not even a stranger exactly. We share a moment, a brief incredulous look of recognition before: Dr. Mongoose asks me what the fuck I'm doing?

Or is it what the fuck do I *think* I'm doing? The second one is better dialogue, but the first feels more natural. Flows off the tip of the tongue and the teeth better. Real Cassavetes shit. He asks again. Louder. "What THE FUCK are you doing in my RV?" Before diving into some sort of high-pitched monologue about respect and boundaries and how you can't just go into somebody's home without their permission.

I am embarrassed, this is true, but I can't seem to move fast enough to properly reflect that. All I can see is a man desperate, frazzled, not King Cool Father to all the wayward hippies like he outwardly attempts to project. An uptight square just like the rest of us. At the end of the day pretending for the show. It's called limits and I just found them.

He's raging with a fury I've seen so pronounced in few before, literally red-faced and figuratively blowing steam, but there's no real fight in him. Not like he's about to kick my ass in the living room of his RV or anything, more like pulling his hair out in a desperate flail. So what's my major motivation to rush out of here when the laughter in my brain is proving to be a suitable replacement for a brokenish heart. If I could only capture his face on a polaroid and look at it every time I needed a boost of inspiration. Hang in there.

Put on the sorry show. Hands up, head down, apologizing ad nauseum as I edge past him and off the bus into the sweet release of fresh air. Sorry sorry so sorry it really was an accident I know you don't believe me as it seems awfully spiteful considering the circumstances and maybe don't go in the bathroom for a while or anything yeah sorry about everything. He's still yelling, but I'm not listening anymore.

Outside, underneath the awning, a few caravanners stare in shock and awe—where did they all come from?—me, the six-headed animal beast from the planet where they leave barn doors open. I shrug. What, like they've never passed out in someone's RV before? For shame. I thought we were all in this together. Brush it off. No big deal. Whateverrrr.

Just kidding. He actually murders me. Good thing my imaginary friend finds my missing keys and avenges my death. Look we did it, the end.

The sun starts to set on my way back to camp. The last visage of daylight playing itself out over the edge of the horizon. The big yellow circle bids it's final adieu of the weekend. Burning gas lowers beyond the hillside. Like a friend waving goodbye on the long walk back to their car. For some reason I stop to watch the whole way through. Might be because they keep waving, or maybe there's inherent value in watching things go. The last little sliver always feels special. Maybe I'm just able to see it a bit longer than anybody else.

§

On the way home we get In-n-Out.

ACKNOWLEDGMENTS

Thank you to Lauren.
To Team Good Vibes and the Party Sharks.
To all who gave their time to make this better:
Tex and Stephen-Paul and Pat and Josh.
And of course to Cavin and Zac.

KKUURRTT is glad you read his thing.
He can be found on twitter at @wwwkurtcom.

BACK PATIO PRESS CATALOGUE

Visit **https:backpatio.press** for more books
and online content. We love you all.
Thank you for reading.

— *Cavin & Zac*

COVER DESIGN

Jacob Burke - @nothingwhateverrrr